the *love* plan

ERICA MARSELAS

Edited by: Kristen @YourEditingLounge

Cover Design by: Sly Fox Cover Designs

This story is dedicated to Melissa, Leslie, Denise, Aakriti, and Lexi because without you guys, this story would have never taken off and come to life. Thank you for listening to me, for all your input, your notes, talking me through—everything. Love you ladies!

Prologue

13 years earlier...

Dexter: 11 years old.

I stand at her door, fidgeting with the edge of my shirt, not knowing what I'm supposed to do. My best friend, Meadow, is wrapped in her pink blanket, clenching the teddy bear I got her several Christmases ago, crying.

Not the kind of crying she does after I steal her toys or even after she falls and scrapes her knee. This is something I've never seen before. Her whole body trembles from under the blankets and she sounds as if she's howling.

Maybe this wouldn't be a good time to ask if she wants to play Guitar Hero?

"Go ahead in, Dex. She needs *you* right now." Valerie, Meadow's mom gives me a gentle squeeze on the shoulder and wipes the tears from her eyes with her other hand. She's the one who had called my mom and told me to come over. I know about some of what happened, but I'm still confused to *why* it happened.

"I don't know what to do."

"Just be there for her. Like you always are. She needs to see that someone else is here and cares for her, other than her old mother."

I slowly walk into her room after a small nudge from Valerie and climb into her bed.

"Meadow?" I shake her shoulder, but she doesn't reply. "Meow, Meow…" I tease her with the nickname I gave her when I was two because I couldn't say her name correctly. It usually makes her laugh and swat at me.

Her head peeks out from under the pink covers, and she wipes away the large raindrop tears with the palm of her hand. "What?"

"I'm here to kick your butt in Guitar Hero." She shakes her head, and I sigh. "Okay, fine, we can do Dance Dance Revolution instead, if you want." I roll my eyes because I hate that game. But I'd play it for her if it'll help her stop crying.

"I don't want to do anything, Dex." She sits up, pulling the blanket and the bear tight to her chest.

"I know." I sling my arm around her shoulder, and she drops her head onto my chest. "I'm sorry about what happened with your dad."

"Why did he give up on me? What did I do wrong?" She cries again, and my shirt wettens from her tears.

"Nothing, Meow." I rub her back. *Why does she think she did something wrong?*

Meadow's mom and dad were never married, and he has been in and out of her life since she was a baby. He used to come around every other weekend, but over the last couple of years, it has maybe only been every other month. I overheard my mom talking to my dad, that he has a new family and signed over his rights. I didn't understand what it meant, but what I did know was that Meadow's dad wasn't coming back this time.

I never liked the man. He always gave me dirty looks and made Meadow cry a lot. And I was never allowed to hang out when he took her to his house. Which didn't seem right because Valerie always lets me come over whenever I want.

It's why I'm so confused; Meadow is awesome. Why wouldn't he want to hang out with her all the time?

"Do you want to try and call Wes?" Wesley is my cousin, and our best friend too. He would want to be here, but he's with my Aunt and Uncle in Florida on vacation

"No...I mean...not yet. He's having fun. I don't want to bum him out." She shrugs and fiddles with the arms of the teddy bear. "I have you...for now."

"You'll always have me. And Wes. I promise."

"You can't promise that. My own dad left!" She cries, now squeezing the bear so hard I'm afraid its head will pop off. "You guys will leave too."

"No, we won't because we're best friends. We love each other, and I promise right now to always be here for you. Forever and ever. No matter what."

"You swear? Forever and ever? You'll always be here with me?"

"I swear!" I declare forcefully.

"You swear on your Jordans and PlayStation 2?"

"I swear on my Jordans and PlayStation and cross my heart, Meadow. Have I ever let you down?"

"No."

3

"Then I'm not going to let you down now. You wanna spit on it?" I spit in my hand and hold it out for her.

Her eyebrows twist and her nose wrinkles. "Dexter, that's disgusting." She shoves me away with her feet and I wipe my hand off on my shirt.

"What? Me and Wes do it all the time." I laugh, and when she giggles, even if it'll only be for a second, I know I did my job.

"I'm not touching either one of you again!" She sticks out her tongue in disgust.

"Yes, you will because you love us." I reach out and grab a hold of her arms to pull her into my lap. She struggles, wiggling around, but she's now laughing harder. I tickle her side making her relent and she collapses into me. "And now you are always stuck with me, Meow."

She smiles up at me and pushes away the last of her tears from her cheeks. "Thank you, Dex."

Chapter One

Present day...

Meadow

"Where's my birthday girl?" my best friend, Dexter, yells from the front door of our townhouse. In his hand, he's flaunting a bottle of Don Julio Tequila, my favorite. I had forgotten to pick up any for the party but leave it to Dex to always know what I need without asking. Another reason why he's my favorite person on this green earth.

"You're late!" I yell back over the lyrics Sia's "Cheap Thrills," blasting through the surround sound, then fall into a fit of giggles. I'm already wasted, having drinks being poured down my throat as if it were my twenty-first birthday and not my twenty-fourth.

"Sorry, babe. Traffic was shit. But you still love me, right?" He blows me a playful kiss and combs his fingers through his perfectly spiked brown hair.

"Forever and ever."

I've known Dexter Greene since I was six months

old and there's still not a day that goes by that I ever tire of seeing his face. *And what a face it is*. I charge for him as he sets the bottle of Don Julio down and loosens his tie. He catches me in his arms without a hitch.

"Miss me?" He chuckles and proceeds to blow a raspberry into the side of my neck.

"Ugh, not anymore." I groan, wiping the mess away as he carries me back to the living room. Our friends look on, smiling; this behavior between us is nothing new for them. *I'm lovesick with my best friend and, well, my best friend isn't*. "You need to catch up. You're behind."

My feet meet the ground again and he bops me on the nose. "I'm not behind, you're just a fucking lightweight."

"Whatever. Mel, get the man his shots." I nudge my girlfriend, who's holding a bottle of Smirnoff. Lined up beside her on the console sofa table is eight filled shot glasses ready to go. She's forever the Bartender. Makes the best drinks and always ready to listen to my problems. "I want him drowning with the rest of us in the next thirty minutes."

"Yes, ma'am." She salutes me and replaces the bottle of Smirnoff with Jack and an empty shot glass.

"Wait!" Dexter holds his hands up. "Before you try to kill me for your birthday, I have your gift in my room. One second." Dexter puts up his index finger and then quickly disappears up the stairs.

"Aww," Mel places her hand on her heart and bats her eyes sweetly, "you guys make my teeth hurt and want to vomit."

6

"Shut up, Mel."

"No, I will not, Meadow," she says pointedly but thankfully makes me what should've been Dex's shot. "I wish you two would just confess your love for each other. Or like bone already. The sexual energy around you two is killing us all."

"Well, I'll make sure to make it my birthday wish. Until then, you are going to have to suffer with me because I highly doubt he'll do either of those."

"If you want, we can tie him down to the bed for you. That way you can have your way with him. Maybe get the whips out and you can ride him into next year."

"Alright, Christian Grey, settle. There will be no tying up or chains or whatever." I throw back the shot and my body shivers as the brown liquor burns all the way down. "If he wanted me, he knows where to find me."

"Ugh, you'll never get anything that way." She picks up one of the tabled shots and tosses it back. "Just let me know if you change your mind. I have rope in the car."

"I'm not gonna even ask."

"Not going to ask what? Why Mel is moonlighting as a serial killer?" Dexter chuckles and slides his arm around my shoulder. "Who we killing?"

"My new coworker." I lie smoothly, though it might not be one. I do want to kill my new co-worker, Kayleigh. But I am not thinking of her and my hands around her neck tonight.

"Oh, okay. Let me know when you need help moving the body." My lips break into a large smile and I wrap my arms around his waist.

I love that I can always count on him to have my back, even when he doesn't know why.

7

"Maybe tomorrow. So, what did you get me?" I ask, noting the wrapped box hanging in his hand.

Dex lifts the box and nudges it into my stomach making me break away from him.

I take the gift from him, feeling giddy. Dexter always gets me the most thoughtful gifts. Peeling back the pink and blue balloon wrapping paper, I reveal a wooden box with a gold clasp.

Tears slip from my eyes as I hold the familiar wooden box. My fingers trace over the faded painted drawings that Dex, his cousin, Wesley, and I drew as kids.

Wesley Greene.

He was our third amigo. He was two years older than us, but we did everything together. Dexter's mother had started babysitting me at six months old, along with Dex who had been nine months old, and Wesley. I don't know how she managed all three of us, but we grew up tight and spent every moment together.

That was till Wesley died when he was eighteen. The three of us were in a car accident caused by a drunk driver. It was—and still is—one of the darkest days of our lives. Wes and I dated for a little over a year and I thought I would have forever with him. Then one day...he was gone. There's not a day I don't miss him, and I know Dexter feels the same way too.

I shake it off, not wanting to remember the heart retching ache now, and undo the clasps of the 'time capsule.'

Right away, I break into tiny giggles seeing the

items we thought we had to preserve forever. Inside is Wes' old Yellow *Power Rangers* action figure and *Indiana Jones* compass. A couple of Dexter's favorite hot wheels, a bunch of colored pictures of Dex's first architectural designs, some letters we wrote to each other, and a mix CD I made.

"I can't believe you found this." We had buried this in the woods behind Wes' house when we were ten. The only problem was we had forgotten to mark where we had hidden it and the area spanned over four acres. I flip over the mix CD I made, and I giggle at the couple of Weird Al Yankovic songs that are mixed in with some classic TLC and Nirvana songs. I had some eclectic taste in music when I was ten.

"It took a while, but Uncle Frank gave me a hand."

"Dex." Words escape me and I throw my free arm around his neck and kiss his stubbly cheek. "Thank you."

"I'm glad you like it. I thought you'd be a little upset you didn't come."

"No, no. This saves me all that digging. And we have it again."

"It's yours...I want you to have my stuff and I know Wes would want you to have his. I have something else for you too."

From his back pocket, he pulls out a white gold chain. I place the box down on the table, and he places the chain in my hand. There's a white gold eternity charm attached to it with little diamonds around it. "Dex, it's perfect." The perfect gift that symbolizes forever and ever. I only wish it meant *more*. That his love for me was more than being friends, *best friends*, and it would lead to him eventually giving me a ring. "Can you put it on me?"

"Of course." He takes the necklace from me, and I spin around and pull up my hair. My body tingles as his fingers brush across my neck to clasp on my necklace. "All done," he whispers in my ear and my head turns, inches from his lips. My lips pucker to give him a quick thank you on his soft inviting lips, but unfortunately, they don't get to make contact when he pulls away, brushing a kiss to my forehead instead.

"Thanks," I smile, trying to keep the disappointment out of my voice.

"What's all this junk?" Julian—Dexter's boss, but also our good friend—breaks up the moment peering into the box on the table.

"It's not junk. They're mementos," I huff defensively.

"Oh, you mean something only you guys will understand. Got it." Julian shakes his head and puts his Coors Light to his lips.

"Yes, pretty much," Dex and I say at the same time.

He chuckles, "I swear you two just need to…"

"Hey, Julian." Mel grabs his arm, coming to the rescue and stopping him from what he was going to say, which I'm sure would have been something to lead to my embarrassment. "We need to get the birthday girl more shots and your buddy boy needs like twenty as well. So, why don't you go fill him up while I set up quarters."

After loading Dex down with his catch up shots, we settle into a game of quarters along with the rest of my friends. I suck at this game. Like legit suck. I suck at it sober and then add alcohol, I suck at it even more. Now being the birthday girl, I'm everyone's choice to drink. My head is spinning, and I'm finding *everything* funny. Like the word moist. There is nothing funny about that cringe-worthy word. But every time Julian mumbles about his quarter being moist, I'm in hysterics instead of kicking him the hell out of my house.

"Dex, can I be on your team?" I plead with a bat of my eyes after I miss the glass...again.

"There's no teams in quarters, Meadow." Steve, my Barney Stinson of sidekick's snorts. "You need to sit there and suffer the drunk consequences."

"I already am *because* you have two faces," I say with an exaggerated slur and hold up three fingers for added humor. Steve flips me off while the others laugh at me. "Now I need someone that can either drink for me *or aim* for me so I can finally pick someone to drink. And it's my birthday *so...*" I shrug and move from my chair and my ass falls into Dexter's lap. Nobody else protests my requests.

Dexter nuzzles his chin into my shoulder and his arm wraps around my waist pulling me in closer. For a moment, it's like we're a couple and not just friends. We're something more and I wish it could stay like this forever.

I wish he could only see how perfect we could be together.

I remember the second I realized I had fallen for my best friend. Honestly, it might have been growing for some time, little by little, and maybe it was always on a low simmer, but it was a year ago when my dog, Pickles, died. Pickles was the dog Dex had bought me after Wes passed. He was this brown chihuahua that looked like Elle's from *Legally Blonde*. I carried him everywhere and, next to Dexter, that little dog helped get me through Wesley's death. I loved that dog, and when he passed, I felt as if I lost another piece of Wes, so I ended up clinging to Dex once again. He carried me around and force fed me for weeks. It all might seem silly, and maybe it's my imagination because Dex has always been there for me through every tough time, but I felt this shift between us.

The looks, the touches felt more electrifying. Every dream he became the star, replacing the Hemsworth Brothers. Even the way we flirted changed to where our friends picked up the sexual energy. I stopped dating and so did he. Every day I've thought about telling him how I feel, but I can't get the courage to do it, in case I'm wrong.

I mean, if he is in love with me, why wouldn't he tell me? Either way, I have him. I have my Dex and it'll happen when it's time. For now, I'll keep doing what I know best...slow seduction...even if it kills me.

"Meadow, Dexter, or whoever...it's your turn." Mel snaps her fingers in my face and chuckles calling me out of my daydream. Dexter laughs in my ear and his warm breath on my bare skin sends a shiver down my spine.

I shift on his lap as I reach for the quarter to give to Dex to take for my turn. He groans and digs his fingers into my hips and his teeth into my shoulder. "Cut it out."

"What?" I play innocent but know it has to do with the sudden bulge in his pants.

He rolls his eyes and grabs his cup, chugging it down, ending his game.

"Well, since Dex is out now." Julian snorts and picks up his red solo throwing it back, also ending his game. "I'm going to hit the head." He gets up from the table and Mel stands, going after him, calling him a slacker for giving up too.

"What did you do that for?"

"Because I think I need more shots, and you could use some food." Dex lifts me in his arms bridal style making me yelp. I throw my arms around his neck and he carries me to the kitchen.

The party has emptied out, and Dex is carrying me on his back up the stairs. "Giddy up horsey," I tease, as he gallops up the final steps. We might be twenty-four, but I think there will always be a part of us that act like giant kids, lost in our childhood, especially after shots of tequila.

And shots of Vodka and Rum and so on....

When we get to the hallway, he puts me down on my feet. My fingers trace the eternity necklace he gave me. "I love this."

"I'm glad. Happy Birthday, Meadow." He tucks a strand of hair behind my ear and his dazzling brown eyes lock with mine.

"Thanks." My lips dry with the words and my tongue darts out to wet them.

"Fuck," he mumbles, leaning into me, and I'm taken by surprise when he kisses me.

And not like any chaste kiss we've shared before. No, this is full possessive, needy, and demanding, as his tongue swirls with mine. His hands roam my body and mine yank at his hair. My feet stumble backward into the wall with a thud, yet our connection doesn't break.

"God, Meadow, this dress..." he mumbles against my lips and in my daze. I can feel his fingers dance along the hem on my dress, inching it up my legs. "I've been thinking all night about how to get it off you."

"You have?" I gulp as his lips descend to my neck and my shoulder and my dress is hiked over my ass.

"Yes, especially when you were shaking this little ass on my lap half the night."

"Sorry." My breath catches in my throat, but I'm

not sorry in the least. This is what I've been waiting for.

"Don't be." His eyes meet mine, darkening, as my dress creeps higher and higher up my body. "Because now I'm going to have my way with you."

"Yes, please."

"Then let's finish getting this dress off you. Arms up."

My arms fly up and my dress goes above my head and then falls to the ground. I'm now standing in front of him in the tiniest of black thongs I own, but he doesn't even take the chance to admire it before he's ripping it off me. It falls, tattered, to the floor as his lips attach to the side of my neck.

"I love you," his voice rasps out the words I've heard him say a million times. Though right now in this intimate, heated moment my heart zaps in an unexplainable way that tells me this is all the *more* I've wanted. *That this* isn't *just the liquor talking.*

My hands tangle into his hair and my hips jerk into his, rubbing against his belt, "I *love* you too," I purr, trying to tell him how *much* I do.

He grunts and his hands move down my back to my ass, and he lifts me in his arms. His lips connect to mine and I'm finding myself carried down the hall, but I'm oblivious of my surroundings till I hit the soft mattress. By the smell of sandalwood and Irish Spring, I know I'm in Dex's bed.

He hovers over me still in his button-down shirt and slacks. "You have too many clothes on, mister." I grab the collar of his shirt and rip it open sending the buttons across the room.

"Eager, Ms. Lexington?"

"Very." I arch an eyebrow and grab for the belt. I struggle to unbuckle it as he attacks my mouth.

Somehow, I manage to undo his belt and slacks and slide them down his ass to free his dick. I fist it in my hand, running my thumb over his thick head, spreading the pre-cum around. For so long, I had always pictured what his thick cock would feel like inside of me, and now it was *finally* happening.

"Meadow, wait." I frown when he moves my hand off his dick. But thankfully, it's only so he can maneuver the rest of the way out of his pants. As soon as he's free he's back to me, kissing me, ravishing me.

This is heaven.

"I love you. Like really love you," he utters with true conviction, making my heart swell. "Like so damn much, Meadow."

"I love you too, Dex. I have, for so long."

His eyes close, and his forehead falls to mine. "Fuck!"

"What? What's wrong?"

"I do love you, but…"

"But what?" I touch his cheek, urging him to look at me, but he doesn't.

He shakes his head, his hair going crazy on top. "I...can't."

He can't?

My heart sinks thinking he's going to turn me down. We're already naked. I'm laying here vulnerable, wanting to give him every part of me and now he's saying no. There's this pain glinting behind his brown eyes I don't understand. He's fighting with something, but what?

What's going through that head, Dex?

"Dex? You can. Please." My hand curls in his hair urging him back to me. "I need you."

"You need me?"

"I need you. Please. Love me, Dex. Make me yours."

His lips mesh with mine again, more eager than before. His dick at my soaked entrance makes me moan and thrust my hips, begging for friction.

I want this. I need this. I'm afraid if I open my eyes it'll all disappear.

"You're so fucking beautiful, Meadow," he murmurs, breaking away from our kiss. His mouth moves to the side of my neck, to my breasts. Sucking and nipping on each of my nipples, making them pebble. "And you taste...god…you taste fucking amazing."

His hand traces down to my center, his thumb finding my clit. "Dex," I whimper when he rubs my sensitive nub and his fingers slide between my soaked folds.

"You're so wet," he groans and sinks another finger inside of me. My legs lift higher up his back, giving him more depth, and I bite the corner of my lip and moan as he hits the right spot. "Damn…that's fucking hot," I vaguely hear him mutter as his fingers pump faster.

"*Ahh,*" I moan, and I unravel around his fingers.

"And that's even hotter." He chuckles, kissing his way back up my body. Once I'm down from my high, his fingers slip out of me and into his mouth, lapping up my juices from them. "*Mmm,*" he hums. "You taste better than birthday cake. Want some?" he says, shoving his fingers into my mouth.

I suck my arousal off his fingers and his eyes darken

hungrily.

"Tell me again how long you have wanted this?"

"For so long. I love you."

"Can you say that again?"

"I. Love. You," I say the words more forcefully, wanting to wipe away whatever worry is weighing heavy on his conscience. He runs his hand down my face before leaning down and devouring me with his kisses and his all empowering love for me.

"You ready for this?"

"So ready," I pant, and his lips consume me once again. My heels dig into his back, and I hold him tighter, as he sinks into me. "Yesssss," I hiss through my teeth as he fills me completely. We fit perfectly. As if we were made for each other.

All right, Meadow, enough with the fairytale mumbo because by the smirk on Dexter's face, he's about to fuck you into oblivion.

"Hold on, baby."

Baby!

My nails dig into his shoulder and his scalp, as his dick pulls out to the tip and slams back in. Our lips find each other again, as the bed creaks and moans below us. His thrusts might be rough, like we're just *fucking*, but his kisses, his kisses are sending me into a tailspin and saying he loves me, cares for me...cherishes me.

"God, Meadow, you feel so damn good," he breathes and recaptures my lips before I can say a word. My moans get lost down his throat and it's as if he is trying to possess me totally.

But I don't care. I'm his.

I buck against him, trying to match his thrusts and take him further. He hits that delicious spot over and over, sending a convulsion to run through me, a tidal wave brewing below the surface.

Dexter moans, releasing my lips to curse silently under his breath. "Roll over."

"Huh?" Before I can say anything else, he slides out of me and turns me over, hoisting my ass into the air.

Well, fuck.

His hand grasps my hip hard, his other hand twisting around my hair, pulling me up. In any other scenario, this would probably hurt like hell, but this…*this is needed.*

"Ready, baby?" My heart soars again at the nickname, and before I can get an answer out, he drives back into me.

"Fuck!" I scream out.

This is intense, more intense than anything I'd ever had before. He's thrusting harder, deeper, and it feels oh so good. My hands grip the sheets for dear life as my body clenches, and I start to see stars. "Dex—"

"Meadow," he pants. "I'm—"

"Yes," I hiss, as my body unravels around him, and the stars I was seeing have now combusted "Dex!"

"Meadow!" He pumps into me, his fingers dig into my hips, as he pours his hot seed into me. "Fuck!"

He slowly pulls out of me and I wince at the absence. I miss it already.

Yup, I'm addicted.

Addictions can be healthy though, in moderate doses…which means every hour of the day for the rest of our lives. Yeah, that would satisfy the craving that's growing in my belly.

He collapses next to me and pulls me into his arms. My head rests on his chest as we both struggle to get our breathing under control. It's only when I start drifting off that I hear Dexter mumbling to himself.

"Dex?" My head lifts, to try to understand what the hell he's saying.

"I can't have you," he murmurs, his eyes closing, and I can feel his body going limp under me. "I can't. You're not mine."

"What are you talking about?" I shake him, trying to have him wake back up and make some sense of what he said, but nothing. He's gone. I sigh and kiss him on his still swollen lips. "I love you, Dex. And you can have me. Forever and ever."

My eyes blink open and there's a slight throb between them. I roll over and I'm met with the naked back of my best friend with his head buried under his pillow. Clearly, our love connection was broken in the middle of the night, but this is also a clear sign Dex is going to be hung the fuck over.

Dexter always covers his head subconsciously in his sleep to block off any chance of light and sound after a night of heavy partying. Add it to the pile of things I find irresistible about him. It's such a silly thing, but when you've known someone their entire lives the little things come extra special.

My finger traces the contours of the muscles in his back, down to his unblanketed sculpted ass. He doesn't flinch and I scoot in closer and trace little kisses along his spine. Still nothing. I bite my lip to contain my giggle and wonder how much longer I'll have to wait for him to wake from the dead.

Though, when my stomach rumbles, I figure I can help both our hangover asses and make breakfast.

But first, a shower.

I'm finishing putting the bacon and sausage onto a plate when I catch a shirtless Dex coming into the kitchen out of the corner of my eye. His hair is standing on all ends and his arms stretch above his head, flexing every ab and stomach muscle.

Fuck, he looks good enough to eat.

My mouth waters and my sex pulsates remembering the way he felt inside of me and how good his kisses tasted.

His brown eyes light up when he sees me and then the plate in front of me.

"Oh yes! Your cure to a hangover breakfast! You're a godsend." He slides onto the stool and stuffs a piece of sausage, wrapped in greasy bacon into his mouth.

"I did." I grin, proudly. "Anything to make sure you're not a zombie all day." I wink and dump my cheesy, onion eggs on to a big plate in front of him.

"That's why you're the greatest!"

"I do my best. Did you sleep well?" I move to sit

beside him and kiss his cheek. His eyes squint at me, but he grins putting the orange juice glass to his lips to take a sip.

"Yeah. I did."

"I did too." I rest my head on his shoulder and inhale the scent of his natural musk. "It was the best birthday I've ever had."

"That's good. I'm glad it turned out well." His shoulder nudges my head, causing me to move away. "You're acting really odd this morning."

"No, I'm not. I'm just...*happy*. Is that okay?"

How could I not be? Our relationship has made the leap I've been waiting for. I figured he would be a little bit more *lively* about it. Want to talk about it— want more of *it!*

"Of course, it is. Sorry. Carry on."

"Good, and you know, I thought maybe..." I draw my finger on his shoulder, acting like this oddball teenager who doesn't know how to flirt, when I consider myself a master on how to flirt with Dexter Greene. "If you want, we could do that again."

"Throw another party of the year. Of course."

"Not the party. What happened after the party. Don't you remember?" My heart is a thumping mess, and my hands start to tingle and sweat.

"After? Like before we passed out? Like did we all do something stupid like when we TP'd Mr. Anderson's lawn." He laughs with the brightest carefree smile on his face.

I don't laugh back.

The ton of bricks of reality hits me and it

tumbles me down that he might truly not remember. Twenty minutes ago, I was lying next to him...naked, and now it's all faded away in the haze of our hangovers.

He has to be messing with me.

Please tell me he's messing with me.

As I stare at him, taking a good look at him, I can honestly say he doesn't have a clue. Because Dexter has never been a good liar. This is the face of a man who is completely clueless; Even though his shiny brown eyes are hazed by his hangover, there's no hint of twitching behind them that he gets when he lies. There's no twinge of sweat or shaky hands.

Meadow, you moron, why did you leave the room? You should've stayed and sucked his dick —not a hangover breakfast.

I just thought I was worth remembering!

"No. It was nothing."

"Come on, tell me. By the time I had those Jägerbombs, man I was gone. It was a fucking good night, Meadow."

Maybe I should tell him. Confess that he said he loved me, that we made love, to where I saw stars. But like another brick being thrown at my already shattered glass house, I remember his final words, *"I can't have you."*

"Meadow, what happened?"

"It really was nothing. I was just shit-faced and I slept in your room. Woke with my foot in your face. I didn't think you would mind, but I know it's been a while since we shared a bed together," I lie but hope it triggers something or he calls my bluff. But all I get is his toothy smile before he sips down the rest of his OJ.

"You always did tend to be a bed hog. Is that all?"

"Yeah. That's all." I swipe a piece of bacon off the main plate.

"You sure?"

"I'm sure." As I bite into the bacon it loses all flavor, turning to dust. I'm angry and sick all at the same time. The beautiful morning I woke up to is now dark and gray and I have no idea what to do.

Chapter Two

Dexter

Meadow is in the kitchen throwing dishrags and dishes around as she tries to 'clean.' It's way too early on a Thursday morning for any of this but it's how it has been all week. The house has become a war zone and I'm public enemy number one. Meadow is the angry Marine out for my blood since the morning after her birthday.

A bowl clatters into the sink with an aggravated groan, and I find myself stepping backward, away from the possible danger zone. If I come into a room, she's ready to eat my soul for breakfast. I've seen all kinds of PMS monsters take over Meadow's body, but this is one of the worst. I've even tried to bribe it with the usual ice cream, heat packs, and chocolate…and all those things were thrown back at my head.

I'm starting to feel as if my best friend hates me. Though I can't figure out why. So right now, I'll avoid her and hope that whatever has taken over my best friend returns her soon.

"Dexter?"

Busted!

"Yes, love?" I mutter sarcastically and bravely step into the kitchen.

Her body freezes at my words, but her eyes narrow, throwing tiny daggers my way.

Yep, I'm about to be chewed and spit right back out.

"You left your spaghetti bowl in the sink, *not* soaking, again. Is it really that hard to put water in it?" she snarls.

"No. I was in a hurry last night. Move and I'll do the dishes." I inch in closer towards her like a gazelle *asking* to get eaten by a lion.

She's a cute little lion though. Her hair is in a tight bun, making her neck kissable, and the tight pencil skirt makes her ass look amazing.

Wait! What the fuck Dex…kissable?

Since when do I check Meadow out like *that?*

Snap out of it. Focus back on trying not to get killed.

See, what's wrong with little Ms. Lion here is everything she's wearing has her wound up so damn tight…

"Dexter!" She snaps her fingers in front of my face. I shake my head, coming back to the reality of the one I'm in and give her a winning smile. "I was talking to you. But not like you listen."

"Sorry. What were you saying?"

"I said I was almost done now anyway." She rolls her eyes, closes the dishwasher with her hip, and then turns it on.

"Why are you even doing dishes before work?"

"I wouldn't have been *if* someone rinsed or soaked his bowl. And cleaning usually destresses me."

26

I bite on my tongue, hard, to the point I might burst a taste bud because that's the furthest thing from the truth. She might think cleaning helps calm whatever evil possesses her or what has her freaking out, when in fact, it doubles the anxiety making her double the crazy.

But I'm not dumb enough to say anything, and the house is always fucking spotless afterward, including my room.

"Right. I get that. Listen, I'm sorry about my bowl and promise not to do it again."

"Pfft. Yeah right."

I take a big risk and grab her waist pulling her to my body. She swats me away with her hand and I grab it with my free hand. "Will you stop beating me up, Meme?" I sneak a kiss on her cheek as she groans, hating one of the many nicknames me and Wes gave her when we were kids. She always hated it because of the *Drew Carey* character with all the makeup and, well, it doesn't fit her.

The only nickname she *allows* me to call her is Meow. But this one is just too good to pass on when she's in a mood like this.

"I'm not going to stop beating you till I knock you out." She raises an eyebrow, and I see a hint of a smile crack on her lips. A sign of the real Meadow breaking through.

"Then I better go before I get hurt. Are you coming for happy hour today?" I let her go and grab my keys off the counter.

"I'll let you know. Depends on how this meeting goes."

"Alright. Later…*Meme*."

"Ugh…you're gonna die," she growls, and the wet

dish towel comes flying at my head. I duck, and it hits the wall next to the door.

"Love you too, babe." I blow her a kiss and her glare at me gets scarier. I make a quick getaway before she makes good on her threat.

Where you at?

I text Meadow, as Lonzo Ball from the Lakers makes a shot on the big screen above the bar, wondering where she could be. It's twenty after five and I've settled into our usual table at *Mike's Tavern* for Thursday Happy Hour. It's our weekly ritual and even if she's acting like the devil possessed, it's not the same without her.

> *Meow: I'm not going to be able to make it tonight. I'll see you later. Tell Randy and Steve I say hey.*

Alright, catch you later.

"Where's Meadow?" Randy asks, smothering his buffalo wing in blue cheese.

"She's not going to make it. But she says hey."

"Oh well, then guys night." He nods, before biting

into his food.

Steve comes back to the table with a beer and a tray of nachos. "Guys night? It's not a guys night without Meadow." He snorts and falls into his chair. "She's the best wingman I got. Who's going to help me with the ladies tonight?"

"Trust me I don't think Meadow would be much help to you anyway. I swear something has taken over her body. Like some voodoo curse." If this is something I have to start going through every month from now on, I might need a new place to live.

Because I'm afraid for my life.

"Well, what did you do to piss her off? Sara always acts insane when I do something wrong even if its load the dishwasher wrong?" Randy peels apart another wing and dips it into the sauce.

"Nothing." I take pause and remember the *small* thing I did do. "*Okay*, I did leave a bowl unrinsed. But it's more than that *and* Sara is your wife. Meadow isn't normally this unhinged over these little things. Like not to the extreme she's been." I chug back my glass of Miller Lite thinking about my insane best friend and wonder if straight-jackets come in different colors for her.

"Meadow might as well be your wife." He chuckles. "But think long and hard. Like at her party, you guys were all over each other. Did you maybe do something? Hook up and then you were so drunk you couldn't get it up? And now..."

The beer pffts out of my mouth. "Noo. Are you crazy? Me and Meadow?"

"Crazy? Dude? You guys...we all had bets going on that you had finally hooked up that night. You sure you guys didn't?"

What the hell? Bets? Sure, Meadow looked good that night, but I would never cross *that* line. It's...*Meadow*.

"I'm sure."

"Well, maybe she was hoping," Randy suggests and digs back into his wings.

"I doubt it. We get flirty, but that's who we are. You know that."

We've always been like that. Nobody questioned or batted an eyelid at our behavior when it would get a little over the top; not even Wes when they dated. It's how we are—a quirky little friendship—and if you couldn't deal, you didn't belong in our circle. Now suddenly everyone is assessing us under a microscope as if something has changed.

"Okay then, I don't know." Randy shrugs. "Maybe ask her what you did wrong. Or sometimes it's easier just to say you're sorry. I learned that a long time ago with Sara."

"The thing is, I did nothing. I want my friend back."

"What you need, my friend, is to get laid." Steve claps my shoulder. "Like I can be your wingman tonight. I learned from the best."

I shove his hand away. "I don't think the techniques Meadow uses for you will work for me. Plus, I'm good anyway."

"You're good?" he snorts, and glances over at Randy and they share a knowing look, snickering.

"What?"

"Neither of us can even remember the last time you dated or even hooked up with someone. Like last month you had that Russian bombshell, who resembled a

30

Victoria Secret model, who actually might have been one. She was all over you. She invited you back to her room and you turned her down because Meadow asked you to pick her up."

I shrug. The girl was hot, but I wasn't into her. When Meadow called it had been the perfect time for me to bail. Plus, Meadow always comes first. "So I was supposed to leave my best friend stranded at some event downtown?"

"No, but motherfucker, one of us would have gotten her. I even offered, remember?" Steve smacks me hard in the arm, and I hit him right back.

I don't know what he's getting all worked up about? He could've taken the chick off my hands for me.

"She asked *me* though."

"That's a fucking excuse. She wouldn't have cared if we got her because you were busy."

Randy nudges Steve's arm with a half-eaten wing in his hand. "Well, she might have because she's in love with Dex." He chuckles.

"Shut the fuck up. It's not like that. And maybe I wasn't into the chick. I hardly even remember her."

"Not into?" Steve scoffs. "She had double DDs to die for and skyscrapers for legs that she was begging to wrap around your head. And you walked away. The Dexter I knew in college would have been all over that and Meadow would have probably helped encourage it in some crazy, weird way, like she does with me. But lately, you two have sworn off the opposite sex. She doesn't date either. She turns down guys all the time when they approach her. So, why can't you admit you want her and then we can all go on our merry way...and I can get my wing woman back."

"You done now?" I have a headache coming on. I only want to enjoy my beer and drop this already.

"No." He grabs his beer and takes a quick sip before flapping on again. "So explain to us what you mean by '*you're good?*'"

"I just haven't been in the mood for one-night stands. That's all."

"Then make them two nights," Steve hoots. "I'm sure that Russian beauty would have taken you around the block a couple of times. Are you saying you want to make them long lasting relationships?"

"I guess." I grab my beer, gulping it down, finding myself annoyed with this conversation.

"So, why don't you and Meadow date if you want the long-term shit?"

I slam my beer down, now pissed. Why are they still trying to push Meadow and me together? Okay, I get we're best friends and we have this connection, but in my heart, she'll always belong to Wes. He loved her until the day he died. The thought of me with her is like breaking bro code.

"When did you two become a bunch of girls?" I joke trying to push away from this conversation and not let my anger get the best of me.

"I'm only trying to understand what's going on with you, man, that's all."

"Well, can we drop it now?"

"Fine. Sorry." Steve holds his hands up defensively and Randy digs back into his buffalo wings.

I throw myself back into my chair and focus on the televisions above the bar. One is playing a Lakers game and the other is playing Meadow's favorite Geico commercial with the camel asking what day it is. As it finishes, I still have no idea what I'm going to do so she'll stop trying to kill me.

"Randy?"

"Yeah?" His head pops up, and he cleans his face off with a napkin.

"What do you do when you need to say sorry...like *really* sorry to Sara even if you aren't?"

Usually, when Meadow and I fight, one of us says sorry or we just get over it. Whatever is going on with Meadow right now, is out of my league, and I need the reserves on this.

Steve hits the table, laughing, and then stands up. "For the love of god, man. You're so whipped and not even getting the pussy. I'm going to get another beer and hit on the hottie waitress. Away from your pathetic ass." He pats my shoulder and I knock him away.

"Shut the fuck up. I just don't want Meadow suffocating me in the middle of the night with my pillows."

"Uh-huh. Keep telling yourself that." He walks away to the bar and Randy is laughing behind his hand.

"Forget this." I stand and reach in my back pocket for my wallet. If I want to be harassed, I'll go home and have Meadow do it. At least there it'll be done in the comfort of my own home.

"Flowers," Randy says simply and I look at him cross-eyed, wondering what he's going on about.

"What?"

"I give Sara flowers. Maybe with candy or a card depending on how deeply I fucked up. Now sit down and chill the fuck out."

I find Meadow on the couch with her feet tucked under her lap, sipping on a glass of red wine. She has the remote in her hand, flipping through the channels, seemingly unaware that I have even come through the door.

Slowly I inch closer to her and clutch the assortment of gas station daisies and lilacs I picked up before I came home under Randy's suggestion. I would have done something nicer, but the flower boutique downtown was already closed for the night. The plastic wrap crinkles in my hand giving me away and Meadow's head snaps in my direction.

"Hey, how was your meeting?" I ask and slide in next to her on the couch. She eyes me curiously at first before she puts her sights on the flowers in my hands.

"It was fine. Would have been much better if I was at the bar with you guys and helping Steve pick up girls, but it was what it was." She shrugs and sets her wine down on the coffee table. "Nice flowers?"

"They're for you." I thrust them into her arms, and she takes them from me. "To tell you I'm sorry."

Her body twists to mine as she places the bouquet to her nose, and eyes me suspiciously over the arrangement. But even through the plastic wrap and the pink and purple petals, I see it; a smile. A genuine Meadow smile that tells me everything might be okay and I'm breaking down whatever wall she's built up.

"You don't even know why you should be sorry."

"Besides my bowl in the sink, no, but at least I finally got you to crack a damn smile. And these did not go flying at my head. So, I say it's a win-win. Am I forgiven for whatever it is I did?"

The flowers fall to her lap and she glances down at them, picking at the rubber band that holds them together. She doesn't say anything for several minutes and I don't know what she could be thinking. I have a feeling she's either thinking over whether to forgive me or maim me with something.

"Meadow, what is going on?" I reach out and brush my hand down her arm, wishing she would tell me. She used to tell me everything that was going on in that head of hers.

Finally, her head pops back up, and a tear runs down her cheek. She wipes it away with the back of her hand.

Shit, I'm in trouble.

"Meadow." I inch closer to her ready to plead for forgiveness. I hate seeing her cry. I only wish I knew what it was I'd done. "What happened? What did I do? It's something. And whatever it is, I'll fix it."

"I have been acting a little nuts, haven't I?" She wipes away another tear from her face.

"A little, but I figured I did something."

Her eyes dart over to the window, a sign she's about to fib, before coming back to me. "It's this new birth control. It's fucking with me. I think I'm going to have to change it back. Even Mel and Steph had mentioned my reign of terror. I'm sorry."

"Why don't I believe that's all of it?"

Her head falls to my shoulder, with a heavy sigh as she plays with the pink petals. "It's also been a shitty week at work. There's this new girl, Kayleigh. She's pissing me off. But you probably don't want to hear about it."

"Of course, I do. Especially if it means you'll stop trying to kill me and direct your anger on someone else now."

She gives a little giggle and scoots in closer to my side. "She's Mr. Hanson's niece and I'm to train her. Teach her everything I know about event planning because he thinks I'm the best to do so next to him. After I train her, he's leaving the company to her. I guess it wouldn't be so bad if she weren't trying to sabotage everything I'm doing. Every idea she claims as hers behind my back. She's been messing with events, canceling things, changing orders. I can't figure out why she's trying to screw me over when all I'm doing is trying to help her."

"Why don't you say something?" My hand brushes through her hair and down her arm. I can feel the tension rolling off Meadow's body, and whatever demon possessed her starts to leave.

I'll have to text Randy and tell him the flowers do work to open a woman up. Though I guess I haven't taken the time to talk or try to listen to her either. Too afraid she might try to cut my head off.

"What's the point? She's already permanently brown nosed her way up Mr. Hanson's ass. I've worked my butt off to get where I am. Now she just walks in and has everything handed to her. Plus, she's got this I'm better than you attitude. I hate her!"

"I'm sorry. I know that can't be easy. But you're the best event planner and Hanson knows this. Maybe you could apply somewhere else?"

"I could, but I shouldn't fucking have too," she snaps and her head goes flying off my shoulder. Oops. I angered the beast. I grab her arm and pull her back, forcing her to my lap.

"Hush, I'm sorry. It was just an idea." I kiss the top of her head, taking a second to inhale the scent of her coconut shampoo. I've always loved the smell of it. "Listen, is there anything I can do? You want me to call Mel? See if she still has that rope in her car? I think I can manage to get my hands on some shovels."

That gets her to laugh, the cute little laugh that makes her snort. The one I love because it's innocent and carefree. She does it when she's trying her hardest not to laugh which causes her to snort, which is why it's my favorite because I know I did it. I feel like I did something right for once.

"You know, I might take you up on that. We could live a life of crime. Become Bonnie and Clyde."

"If anyone could pull it off, it'd be us." I chuckle, and she wraps her arms around my waist and places her head back on my shoulder.

"Too bad our parents would end up finding us before the cops and kill us first."

Our mothers always had a way of finding out when we caused any kind of trouble. They were bloodhounds. Even once we got away for college.

"You're probably right. So, are we okay now?" I lift her chin, having her look at me. Her green eyes still clouded from her tears. I want to push her to tell me more of what she's hiding because I know it's more than birth control and Kaylee or whoever. But I know she'll tell me when she's ready. "Are you going to stop trying to kill me?"

"I guess so. I mean the flowers are pretty nice."

Wonder if she'll still feel that way knowing that I got them from the Exxon across the street from the bar. "Only the best for you. You still love me? Even though I didn't soak my bowl?"

"Forever and ever."

Chapter Three

Meadow

Staying mad at Dexter has never been my thing. It's impossible, especially when he's not aware of what he's done wrong. He had been super drunk. Twice as much as I was. And it had been my dumbass fault for leaving him alone and also for not telling him what happened. I have to take my own responsibility for that.

There is a part of me that perhaps knows where Dexter's mind was that night, where his hesitation stems from: it's because to him, I'll always be Wes' girl. That's what I've always been. Even after Wes' death when I started dating again my sophomore year of college, he frowned upon it. Always questioned every guy's intention like this crazy big brother.

It always drove me insane, but I allowed it because I knew it came from a good place. He'd promised to take care of me and that's what he had been doing.

Instead of stewing in my anger I go for a different tactic and devise a plan. I figured I had one of two choices. I could either tell him—which is no fun at all and comes with a huge risk of being rejected and our friendship taking a hit.

And that's the last thing I want.

So, that only leaves me with my second choice. The fun route. I call it: The Flirt.

For many years, I've watched women flaunt over this man and shake what they have, which landed them in bed with him. Usually, it was a shake of the ass or a laugh that was too loud or screechy. Now, Dex isn't a man whore, he doesn't sleep with every woman he meets. But he's not always necessarily picky either. I have no idea what he saw in most of the women he'd slept with, but at the time it wasn't my right to judge, nor did I care.

Well, except over this last year.

Thankfully, he hasn't been bedding many women lately. *Which I took to mean he was having the same feelings for me that I was for him.*

The one thing Dex and I have going already is that we know how to flirt with each other. It's something we've been doing since we were in diapers. It comes naturally. Now, what I have to do is up my ante and take off more of my clothes and maybe bat my eyes a bit more.

Hell, I'm not even sure. I'm winging this.

My first step in my plan is what I dub as the nightmare.

It's a key seller in porn. And Dex will never say no to me if I'm having a nightmare. At least I hope not. After Wes died, I found myself in his bed all the time. Back then, there wasn't anything ever sexual about it He had been my security blanket and I think I was his too. *Now it was time to change all that.*

I slip into a pair of red allover lace boy-shorts and a

white silk camisole. I want to look hot, but not overdone. I tend to wear plaid pants and oversized shirts to bed. If I wore this every night I would freeze, and I'm not trying to impress my blankets, but I've never had to try so hard with Dex. Nor did I think I would have to try this hard now.

I move across the dark hallway, turning on my phone to light my path. In part, I feel like such an idiot for doing this, but a girl has to do what she's got to do. He's asleep on his back with one arm above his head and the other across his chest. His mouth is parted and he's snoring softly. I pull back the covers to reveal him only in a pair of black boxers. It isn't fair how perfect his body is. His wide shoulders, his well-defined abs with that drool worthy *V*. But I guess he has worked for it. He's always been a gym nut and ran track and played lacrosse in high school. Then after Wes died, Dex used exercise as a way to fight his aggression and a way to deal, which added to the layer of muscles.

I lay my phone on his nightstand and crawl into his bed and snuggle into his side. My arms wrap around him and I lay my head on his chest listening to the sound of his beating heart. I inhale the crisp scent of his Irish Spring soap. The night of my birthday comes back to my memory. The touches, the kisses, the way he felt inside of me. I want that connection again. If only there were some serum to help his blackout memory.

He hasn't flinched since I came in here. He's always been a bit of a heavy sleeper. I snuggle in closer and rub my hand along his six pack. My eyes start to droop, and I place a kiss in the center of his chest. "Love you, Dex, ever and ever."

Of course, out of all the things I have done, it's the kiss that makes him startle. "What are you doing?"

"I had a nightmare." I yawn and curl further into his side.

"What are you? Five? Go sleep in your own bed."

"No. Please, Dex. You never cared before."

"Well, do you have to sleep right on top of me?" He squirms, peeling me off his body. "And why are you naked?"

"I'm not naked, you goof. I have clothes on. Please!" I beg. "It was really bad. It was about that night with Wes. And you're so cozy, and you always make me feel safe."

I shouldn't have gone there. It had been the first thing that popped in my head. It's evil and I do feel dirty for even claiming it, and maybe I will spend my end of days in Hell for it. But in an instant, I'm pulled back into Dex's strong arms and he kisses the top of my head. "Fine, you can stay. Just stop moving."

Wesley would forgive me. He would want us together.

Though for some reason this knucklehead can't see it.

"Thank you, Dex."

"Yeah, yeah, yeah. Now sleep."

I wake up warm and entangled in the arms of the man I love. Pressed between my legs and digging deliciously into my sex is his impressive morning wood. I'm soaked and use the opportunity of having him so close to me to wiggle my hips against his dick for some friction.

I'm pleased when he grip's my ass pulling me tighter and groans. At least in his dream-like state he wants me.

"Dex," I say his name like a prayer hoping that he'll subconsciously hear my need for him.

"Meadow…" My prayer is answered when he whispers my name back.

"Yes." I kiss the tip of his prickly chin and trace my nails down the side of his stomach along the hem of his Calvin Klein's.

It's the moment I know I went too far when his eyes fly open, wide in fear. He pushes my body away as if I'm a rabid dog. He shoots out of the bed, falling to the floor, taking the sheets with him in the process. His reaction is laughable but at the same time crushes a piece of my heart.

"Geez, Dex. It's just me."

He stands back to his feet, throwing the blankets to the bed, covering me up, making me laugh harder. "I knew that."

He scavenges around looking for something and I bite my lip noticing he's still erect.

I want to reach out and put my hand around it…then my mouth.

"Meadow!" Dexter snaps, drawing me away from a perfect daydream.

"What?"

"Stop...*looking*..." he grits out. A hint of pink

appears on his cheeks as he slips on his gray sweatpants.

My giggles return at his sudden shyness around me. "Chill out! You act as I've never seen *it* before."

I've seen Dexter Greene naked more times than I can count, granted the only time it counted was on my birthday.

His mouth opens then closes before he scrubs his hands down his face. "I'm going to take a shower."

"Alright, have fun," I call out as he moves nervously towards his bathroom.

I fall back to his pillows glancing up at the ceiling. Well, that plan was a bust.

We were so close, he muttered my name in his sleep, and still, I'm treated as if I have cooties.

My head turns to the clock on his nightstand, and I note it's a little after eight. I guess I can cook us breakfast...while also giving him an extra glimpse of my *special* nightwear.

I busy myself in the kitchen, turning on my favorite Spotify playlist, to make breakfast for us. They say the way to a man's heart is through his stomach. Well, I've been cooking my way into this man's heart since college. Now, there's no doubt that I have it, now if only I could have him completely heart, body, and soul, that would be even better.

I'm so lost in the lyrics of Pink's "Beautiful Trauma" and singing along that I don't notice Dex come into the kitchen till he clears his throat behind me.

I peek my head over my shoulder and give him a flirty smile. "Mornin' again." I hold back my laugh at his appearance. His hair is still dripping wet from his shower and he's put on what appears to be an extra layer of clothing. I see a pair of basketball shorts peeking underneath his sweatpants and he's also wearing an oversized hoodie. "Cold?"

"Where's the rest of your clothes?" he croaks, avoiding my question.

"In my closet."

"You're such a smartass. I'm serious. Since when do you cook in your underwear?"

"This isn't my underwear. They're called *pajamas*."

"And since when do you wear pajamas that look like that?" He runs his finger up and down my body and I smirk when I notice his eyes linger on my ass a tad longer then they should.

I shrug. "Since now? Don't you like them?" I spin around and let him get the full view of my ensemble.

He clears his throat and mumbles, "They're fine," before he moves to the refrigerator.

At least, I know that I affect him. I go back to the griddle and hear him rattling around in the fridge behind me as I flip the blueberry pancakes and bacon.

His favorite.

"Do we have any more of those Mountain Dew Kickstarts?"

"No, I think you drank them all. In fact, we don't

have much of anything in here. We should probably go to the store if we don't want to live off take out all week."

"Yeah, we can go after our hike." He sits at the breakfast bar and I can feel his lingering eyes on me as I place the pancakes on the serving plate.

Bootylicious begins to play, and I turn up the volume to blast the song through my phone speakers. "Oh, I love this song." I move around the kitchen to grab some cups and more plates. Though as I'm doing so, I channel my inner Beyoncé and shake my ass to show off for the guy at the bar. I just might not be as graceful as the queen herself.

Dex clears his throat, and I whip my head around, so my hair goes flying. "Now what are you doing?"

"Dancing." I laugh and set the plates down on the bar.

"What you are doing is *not* dancing."

"No? Then what is it then?"

"It looks like you're having a seizure." He steals a piece of bacon and walks out of the room.

"Hey, don't you want pancakes?" I yell after him, wondering where the hell he's going. I'm going to be pissed if all this food goes to waste.

"Yeah!" he calls back, "once you stop scarring me with those lame dance moves."

"Asshole!"

Dex and I finished a ten-mile hike up in Cronan Ranch Park. Hiking is one of the things we started doing when we were teens. The whole world around us is forgotten. All troubles are set aside and for those couple of hours, it's just me and him. I love hiking with him.

Going grocery shopping with him, not so much. He's a pain in the ass when it comes to the chore. Like I become the mother, having to control their child from putting everything into the cart. I use the word 'no' way more than I should. Case in point, Dexter is grabbing two large bags of French fries from the large freezers and then throws them into our cart.

"What are you doing now? We don't need those."

"Says who?"

"Me."

He ignores me and turns back to the freezers to grab three personal pizzas and throws them into the cart on top of the fries. He's never going to eat those. They're only going to collect ice in the back of the freezer.

"Dex!"

"What?"

"Put those back!"

"No."

"Yes."

"Tell me one reason why I should?"

My finger darts out and I poke him in the stomach like he's the Pillsbury Doughboy. Instead of hitting something soft and squishy I hit a wall of muscle. "Because you're getting a little pudgy around the edges."

"Did you just call me fat?"

"I didn't say...*fat*... just that you have a little pudge coming in." I joke and when I go to poke him again, he

47

swats my hand away. He turns back to the freezer and grabs another bunch of frozen dinners, causing me to break out in a fit of laughter. "Oh my God. You nutball."

"Hey, you only live once. Plus, they're good."

"Don't come crying to me when you have to go to the gym to work it off."

"You know, it's no wonder people think we're married."

"Who says that?" My laughter stops. Where did this random thought come from?

And why does he sound so annoyed by it?

"Who doesn't?" he argues back, baiting me, and I cross my arms over my chest.

"I've never heard it."

Lies, oh the lies. I've heard it said a million times, not that I mind.

He rolls his eyes and throws his arm over my shoulder, kissing the top of my head. "You're so full of shit. I know for a fact Mel said it to you the other day." Dex grabs the cart with his right hand and pushes it down the aisle along with me. "I mean how much more cliché can we get than grocery shopping together on a Saturday? Like, isn't this what all the tied down people do together? Like some kind of ritual."

"I wouldn't know. And maybe if you didn't eat all the food, we wouldn't have to be here all the time."

"You're the one always cooking for my ass."

"Well, someone has to or you'd starve." I giggle and pat his sexy, firm tush that I wish I could sink my teeth into. He plants another kiss on top of my head and breaks away from me to the freezer. This time grabbing some frozen veggies.

"What would you think about us getting a roommate again?"

Okay. Whoa. Back the train up. What the fuck is going on?

A roommate? Has he lost his damn mind?

We should be making all these steps forward and now I suddenly feel we've made a million steps back.

"What? Why?"

"I thought maybe it would be good to have someone else help with the rent. It worked well when Mel and Steve lived with us before."

"Yeah, because they were our besties and even they got sick of us."

They got sick of us *real fast.* Mel lived with us for only four months before we drove her insane and Steve made it about six.

"*Because,*" he stresses, "they think we're some annoying married couple…all the rules…and shit…and set in our ways."

"I don't want anyone else. I like only us in our house." I'm doing my best not to whine and stomp my foot like a spoiled brat. But right now, he's out of his damn mind if he thinks I'm going to have anyone come into my house.

"I think it'll be nice to have someone else around again. It could be fun."

"Couldn't we get a puppy again? Maybe one for each of us this time. It would be nice to be fur parents again."

His eyebrows twist, looking at me as if I'm insane. "*Oh*, because that would really help with anybody thinking we're not married."

"What's the issue anyway?" I grab the cart and shove

it down the aisle away from him. I'm finding myself offended because this shit never bugged him before. We always laughed it off, even before my feelings developed into more. "You never cared if I said those things before."

"Nothing," he chuckles, catching back up to me. "It was just an idea. I only want you to think about it."

I needed to vent. I needed to scream. Hell, I needed to punch something, but I settled for liquor at Roxann's with Mel and Steph. This is where we usually go to sing Karaoke every other weekend, but now the only song I was singing was a swan song as I gave up on convincing Dex he loved me.

"He wants me to think about getting another roommate. Do you guys believe this?"

"I totally could get on that…" Steph holds up her finger with a grin eager to take me up on the deal.

"No," I snap, folding her finger down.

"Hey!" Steph frowns. "I'd be the best roommate ever."

"Not like that. I love you, but I don't want anyone else coming in on my Dex time."

"You are such a greedy little thing," Mel snorts with a roll of her eyes. "Your *Dex time* because you don't already have him hogged tied for yourself."

"What is with you lately and all the tying down references?"

"I discovered kink. When you finally hook up with Dex *again*, I'll loan you some books." Mel nudges me. I can only imagine the reading material she has on hand.

"Well, you might be waiting forever. I've done everything I can think of to try and turn Dex's head and he still only thinks of me like some sister."

"Why not use the words. Hey, Dex, I LOVE YOU. They would be so much easier."

"Yes, but…"

"But nothing. He does love you." Mel grabs my hand. My eyes close and I'm hit with the vision of that night—the pain in his eyes when he was over me telling me he *can't* love me.

"I'm not sure. Yeah, he told me in a drunken confession that he was *in love* with me, but even his drunk confession was doubtful. I'm not sure sober Dexter is aware."

"What do you mean?" Steph asks curiously.

"I thought a lot about it. And when he mentioned not being able to have me, I think it has to do with Wes."

"Wes?" Mel stutters baffled. "But Wes has been gone for seven years…"

"I know, but I don't know, to Dex I was and have always been Wes' girl. He always got weird when I dated again. It's just my guess. I'm afraid if I say anything to Dex and he blows me off or says he really doesn't feel the same it'll change everything. Or admit to him we did sleep together and it makes him mad. I don't want to lose my best friend. I want Dex to realize for himself he loves me. I don't think that's so wrong, is it?"

"And what if he doesn't?" Steph asks.

"At least I always have him." I shrug. Yet, as I say the words, I'm not totally convinced that it's enough.

"What if we gave him a push?" Mel snaps her fingers and I swear a light bulb just lit up above her head.

"What are you talking about?"

"Oh come on. I'm talking about every single cliché romance movie and book ever written. We get Dexter to see what he's missing. You haven't dated since you got lovestruck with him, so maybe it's time you did. Make yourself unavailable—and then, ding, he's gonna want what he can't have."

"And how do we pull that off? I don't know anyone that I could just use like that."

"Oh, I think we do. And he so happens to be good friends with Dex too." Mel grins.

My mind goes through our list of friends, of who the hell she could possibly be thinking of, and I'm coming up blank. "Who?"

"Julian."

"Julian? As in Dex's boss? No way." I love Julian, but he's not my *type* and I doubt Dex would believe it.

"Yes, way. He'd be perfect for this. He was with us when we were all laughing it up about how hard headed you two were about your feelings for each other at your birthday party as you two dry humped in the middle of your living room."

"Wait! You guys were talking about us?"

"Yeah. You two are like this little mini soap opera for us." Mel cackles, and Steph nods in agreement. Yeah. I guess we are pretty dramatic. "Anyways, now that we know there's more to this story. We want to help."

"Okay, but wouldn't it be better with someone we don't know."

"I think it would work better with someone that would be okay with being duped, don't you think?" Steph chimes in, before taking a sip of her margarita.

"I guess, but why Julian? They work together."

"Okay, so Julian's name sort of pulled out of my ass. But he's awesome. And he's what I like to call a panty charmer. You know him. We all know him. So, it's not like you would have to do anything, and I totally know he would be on board to mesh you two lovesick crazies together." Mel grins, clapping her hands. "It'll be great."

"Fine, I'll try anything at this point. But only if he's onboard, and you're calling him."

"Hello, ladies." Julian gives us his panty-dropping smile as he slides onto the stool between me and Mel. "You wanted to see me?"

"We have a proposition for you," Mel starts, grabbing his hand.

"A proposition, huh?" Julian's gray eyes suddenly gleam, and his full white smile grows bigger. Steph groans, mumbling 'boys' under her breath.

"Get your mind out of the gutter." Mel swats him playfully. "Meadow needs you to play Romeo to make

Dexter absolutely mad with jealousy so he can get his head out of his ass and admit how he really feels about her."

He blinks at her for a second, absorbing her words, then chuckles. "Okay, so let me get this straight. You want me to pretend to go out with Meadow, in hopes to open up Dexter's eyes that he's in love with her?"

"Pretty much," I say softly with a heavy sigh. It all sounds so easy, but it probably will be anything but.

"Why don't you just tell him?" He looks at me curiously, making Mel and Steph moan. I glance at them wondering if I should tell him the details. "What?"

I recite what happened the night of my birthday, from the hookup and then Dexter being so blackout drunk that he forgot. "And I don't know. I think if I told him, he'd find some excuse not to."

"I see. Well, I'm glad to see you're both not oblivious to your feelings. I'm in."

"Really?" I'm surprised how easy he accepts. I thought I was going to have to bribe him with cash or even flash my boobs…or something.

"Yeah. Could be fun fucking with Dex. When do you want to start?"

Chapter Four

Dexter

"I need you to fax these designs and specs over to Mallory and then you can go," I tell Joyce, my secretary. She reminds me of Sophia Petrillo from the Golden Girls. She's tiny, with white curled hair and big rimmed glasses, and she sasses me *all* the time. *Yes, I know the Golden Girls thanks to my mother and Meadow.*

It figures Julian, my man-whore of a boss would get Amber—a Secretary with legs for miles and boobs like Pamela Anderson—and gives me grandma as a way to fuck with me, but it just so happens that Joyce is amazing at her job and efficient—unlike Amber. In the end, I'm eternally grateful for Joyce.

"I'll get right on it, Mr. Greene." She smiles and turns around to walk back to her desk.

Rounding the corner is Meadow, in a tight black dress, making her legs look like hot sin and her breasts are practically spilling from the short neckline—*holy shit*! My dick twitches and I find the need to adjust myself.

What the hell? Again, I'm checking out Meadow like

I would some random hot babe at a bar.

Like this is Meadow.

My Meadow. Wes' Meadow.

Why is she dressed like this?

It's bad enough she had me jacking off in the shower the other morning when I woke up after she slept in my bed. Now, I don't think it was her *per se*, but it didn't help my normal morning wood was pressed into her, and the wiggling and the moaning did nothing to help matters. Or the way she was eyeing my dick.

Then why did I only think of her and call her name as I came?

"Don't you look pretty!" Joyce stops her and looks her over. "Hot date?"

"You could say that." Meadow grins, tucking her auburn hair back behind her ear.

Joyce glances over her shoulder at me and clucks her tongue in disapproval. "Well, Dex, you better get going. Call the fairy godmother if you want a chance to compete with this beauty tonight."

"Watcha talking about? I'm fine." I wave her off and uncomfortably fix my navy checkered tie with the other hand.

Meadow giggles and squeezes Joyce's shoulder before walking my way. When she's in front of me she grabs the lapels of my Burberry suit and I take a second to inhale the scent of her honey blossom perfume.

"Where are we going that you're so dressed up for?"

Her eyes widen and she chews on her lower lip. "Oh, umm, not we. I'm actually here for Julian."

"Julian?" I question, making sure I heard her right. "Julian St. James? My boss? The owner?"

She's going out with him? Dressed like that? Without me? I don't fucking think so.

"Yeah. One and the same." She laughs. "Also known as our friend. We're going to dinner at SoHo and then seeing the new Avengers movie."

"We were supposed to see that," I snap. I'm not okay with this. We planned to see that movie months ago— we've already seen the rest of the series together.

She frowns. "I didn't think you would mind because I figured you and Steve would be going to see it anyway. I'm sorry."

"Well, I could just tag along."

"It's kind of a date, Dex," she confirms what I already knew, but it doesn't make me feel any better.

"A date?" I spit the word out, trying to get rid of the bitter taste in my mouth.

She hasn't been on a date since god knows when, and she's going out with someone she once called a fuckboy?

"Yeah. He asked me out."

"He did? When?"

Why the hell is she just telling me this now?

"Yesterday. I said yes. It's been a while since I've been out. And Julian is nice."

"He's not your type, Meadow," I grit out, no longer being able to control my temper.

"What do you mean?"

"He uses women like they're disposable. He's just going to end up dumping you in a couple of days. You should just call it off, or I could come with you." I try to reason with her.

"That's not a nice thing to say about our friend, Dex. And I don't need a babysitter."

"You've said the same thing yourself," I argue.

"Well, I've changed my mind," she huffs. "I've seen a different side of him. He's really not that bad and he treats every girl he dates right."

"But you're talking about dating Julian St. James. It's not like you're only going out and having a beer. As your best friend, it's my job to tell you it's a bad idea."

She's out of her mind! I want to shake her in the middle of this hall because it seems all her common sense is missing.

"You're telling me this as my friend, huh?" She raises her eyebrow at me.

"Yeah."

"Oh, and nothing else?" She grabs my tie and wraps it around her hand. Now I'm confused by this change of direction she has going on here.

"What?"

"You sound like a jealous ape instead of a best friend." She smirks and jabs her finger in my chest.

What is she getting at? I'm not jealous. It's my job to take care of her. To look after her.

"I'm not jealous. I know what Julian is like. You know what he's like. And honestly, I'm not going to deal with you all heartbroken for weeks over him when you know better."

"You're being an asshole," she growls and pushes away from me. "You know that. I'm a big girl. I can go out with whoever I want."

"You can. Just not Julian!"

"You've said this about Mark, Cody, and Santino." I roll my eyes at Santino's name. Her college boyfriend and first boyfriend after Wes. He was the worst of them all.

They only dated for a few months till she caught him cheating, and guess who had to be the one to help her pick up the pieces?

Me.

"See, you can't even keep the dirty look off your face at their names. All of them not good enough for some reason or another."

"And I always ended up being right."

She rubs her temple with her forefingers and sighs. She can't deny that I'm right. "You never heard me give this much hate on any girl you've dated."

"Molly," I say smugly of an ex-girlfriend I dated for about six months two years ago. "Because you so happened to *love* her."

"You hush your mouth about that bitch." She smacks me in the chest, hard enough it stings.

"Damn, settle. Sorry." I rub the spot where she hit. Okay, so Molly is a sore subject, especially for Meadow. While the relationship started off good, near the end Molly went out of her way to do everything to try to break up Meadow's and my friendship. At one point, she got close. Molly had made up lies saying that Meadow was threatening her because she had thought she was coming between us. Then, at one point, she played that Meadow had attacked her. I almost believed Molly, but thankfully I knew Meadow better. Molly's lies came to light and I kicked her crazy ass to the curb.

I like to think the experience brought us closer.

"Don't you ever say that name again!" she hisses. "That *harlot* doesn't come close to Julian and you know it. Now, what's really going on?"

"It's just I happen to know what's good for you."

"What seems to be good for me is being single forever."

"I didn't say that." I sigh, but yes it probably would be best. Though, I'm not dumb enough to say that out loud.

I'd like to keep breathing.

"Everything okay, you guys?" Julian walks up behind Meadow and slides his arm around her shoulder, making my blood boil. He's already marking all over her before they go out on a date?

"Everything is fine." Meadow plasters on a fake smile and slides her arm around Julian's waist. "We should go so we don't miss the movie." She pulls him away down the hall.

"You won't miss much. I heard most of them disintegrate at the end anyway," I call out the huge spoiler I read from the rotten tomatoes site. "Then you have wait for the next one."

Meadow shoots me a fiery glare over her shoulder, and I give her a smug grin before she disappears.

Now that seeing the Avengers is in the dust, and rather than wait for my best friend to come home with her heart broken, I'll go visit my mother and father.

Really living it up, Dex.

Though there's a good reason behind it. In a couple of weeks, my parents along with Meadow's mom are throwing Wesley's parents a 35th wedding anniversary party and there are a couple of things to discuss. Meadow and I are doing everything to help.

I pull up to my childhood home where the tire swing still hangs from the giant oak. I would spend hours pushing Meadow in that damn thing. Some days, I attempted to spin her around enough to the point where she couldn't stand up or even where she would get sick. Wes, on the other hand, would tend to look on as he read on the porch.

My house was the main meet up spot because it was between Meadow's and Wes'.

There are times—actually, it's all the time—where I wish I could go back in time and bring Wes back.

I pull out my key, but before I get it into the knob the door flies open. "Dexter!" My mom greets and pulls me into her arms. "What are you doing here? Did I miss your call?" She leads me into the house and closes the door behind us.

"No. I thought I'd stop by and bring over the recommendations for those catering dishes you were asking about for the party."

"Oh, thank you." She takes the list out of my hands and glances over it. "Where's your other half?"

"Huh?"

"Meadow?" She laughs. "You never walk into this house without her attached to you. I figured she'd be with you. So, where is my sweetie?"

"What, am I not enough?"

"Did I say that?"

"Basically."

"You know it goes without saying Meadow is my favorite Monday, Wednesday and Sundays. And it's Wednesday. So, where's my girl?"

"Thanks, Mom. I can just go." I point back to the door.

"No. No. I'll just put in a trade." She wraps me in her arms and kisses my cheek. She quickly looks me over and touches the spot she kissed. "But really, where is she? This is twenty years of routine you're breaking. Are you fighting? I figured she'd be the one bringing me the list since it is what she does for a living."

"No. She's out on a date. With *Julian,*" I hiss. I'm actually fucking hissing the name of someone I consider my good friend because he's probably got his hands all over the one I consider my best.

I hate it. I want to break his hands.

"Your boss? I thought you liked him."

I did until he asked my best friend out behind my back.

"He's fine. I mean yeah." I shrug.

"*But?*"

"He's not right for Meadow."

"*Ohhh.* I see." She smirks and fidgets with her necklace.

"What are you getting all up about?" I roll my eyes. If anyone is going to try to make mountains out of molehills or try to turn shit to gold, it's going to be my mother.

"You're finally admitting how you truly feel," she says, seeming positively giddy with herself like she guessed the final question on Jeopardy.

"Oh my god, what is with everyone lately? Meadow is like my sister and it's my job to make sure she doesn't end up hurt."

"And you think Julian will hurt her?"

"Yeah."

My mom taps her chin, making a humming noise, a sign that she doesn't believe me

"It's true," I argue, feeling as if I'm on trial.

"I know Julian, and I don't believe it for a minute. He's kind and I think he would treat Meadow like she deserves. I think it's only because you don't want them together and not because of *who* he is."

"That's not true."

"Oh, your denial river runs deep, son."

"I'm not in denial." I shake my head and yank on my hair walking into the living room. My mother follows yacking it up behind me. If only Dad were home maybe I would have someone on my side. "I'm glad you find my life a comedy show."

"I don't know why you're acting so scared." She sighs and places her hand on my shoulder.

"I'm not," I mutter. Out of the corner of my eye, I spot a picture of Meadow and me on the mantel from last Christmas. We're both wearing ridiculous Christmas sweaters and her head is on my lap, looking up at me smiling. Then beside that picture, is a framed photo of her with Wes. I walk over and pick it up and stare at it. Studying how she's looking at Wes to how she looks at me and for a fleeting moment, I swear it's identical.

I remember the day my mother snapped the picture of her and Wes. It was about a month before we lost him. We were out in the backyard, having a graduation party for Wes. He was a year ahead of us and was going out to Washington State University in two months. Unfortunately, he would never make it. My heart twists and my eyes close, as I go back to that day, one of the last good days before he died…

I groan and pinch the bridge of my nose watching my two best friends make out in front of me—again. I should be used to this affection, *but after a while it gets old. I'm happy for them and what not but wouldn't mind going back to the days I wasn't a third wheel and I could hang out with them without the slobber noises.*

"You two done yet?"

Meadow pulls away from Wes and she blushes. She always did look so cute when she got all shy, even now, after making out with Wes.

"For now." She shrugs and tucks a loose hair behind her ear. "I'm going to grab a soda. Do you two want one?" she offers.

I ask for a Coke and Wes asks for the same.

She bounces back into the house, and I throw myself back in the lawn chair looking at my other best friend who is still wearing a shit-eating grin from that kiss he got.

"God, you two make me nauseous."

"You're just jealous you can't have what I have."

He grins glancing back at the house making me roll my eyes. He and Meadow have been dating for over a year, and though she's still in high school it wouldn't surprise me if Wes proposed to her when she graduates next year. They'll go the distance and I'll more than likely be single forever in their shadow.

"Whatever."

"I hope one day you can have it."

"Kind of hard when all the girls I date are afraid of Meadow even though she's with you."

Any girl I end up with will have to understand that Meadow is a part of my life and isn't going anywhere. The one thing I can't handle is crazy jealous chicks.

"You'll find her. You'll have to stop being so hard-headed and let her in."

"Whatever. I'm fine. Unlike you, I much rather go out and have fun. Meet all the ladies. I don't need to 'settle down.' Why should I have to anyways when I can live vicariously through you two?"

"Okay, *now* I understand." My mother's voice and tight clasp on my shoulder brings me back from the past.

"Understand what?" I glance at her confused, wondering what the hell she's talking about now.

"Why you won't go after Meadow. It's because of Wes. You know he wouldn't…"

I drop the picture back down and step out of my mother's grasp.

"*Wes* has nothing to do with anything because there isn't *anything,*" I stress, hoping she'll get the point that I don't have some *deep hidden feelings* for Meadow. "Please stop pushing this."

"Fine, fine. I'm sorry. I only want you to be happy, you know that. I'll drop it." She puts her hands up and steps back. But knowing my mother, this won't be the last of it. This is only the beginning. Soon Valerie and Aunt Martha will be joining the ranks of this conspiracy. "Now, would you like to stay for dinner. Your dad should be home shortly. I made one of your favorites, pork chops."

I smile, and my mouth waters—nothing will make me forget like my mother's cooking.

I jiggle the door handle and open the door to a sea of darkness. I'm disappointed that Meadow is still not home. I drop my keys on the counter and flick on the light. Moving to the fridge, I grab a beer and settle onto the couch to wait for her. Why am I waiting for her? Torturing myself? Maybe I should be like Steve and go out and find a woman to pick up, go to her place and lose myself in her. Hell, when was the last time I even did that? I try to wrack my brain to remember and I can't. I can't even remember the last time Meadow went out with someone.

But now knowing that she's out with Julian and his hands could be all over her body—in that dress she was wearing—that dress she looked fucking irresistible in...

Shit!

My dick grows and strains against the zipper. What the hell is going on with me lately?

I adjust myself and throw my beer back, then stand to get another one. Trying everything to wipe away the image of Meadow in that fucking dress and how good her legs looked.

And stop picturing them wrapped around me.

Shower! I need a shower!

A *fucking* cold one!

She's still not back when I get out, and I'm not feeling any less antsy either. I run my fingers through my damp hair and pour myself a shot of Jack.

It shouldn't be driving me this insane. Julian isn't that bad, but he isn't good enough for her.

Nobody ever will be.

Nobody can be Wes.

I throw back the shot and let it burn back the bitterness bubbling in my throat.

The time ticks by. I pace and flip through channels as I wait for her to come home. Finally, a bit before eleven I hear the rumble of what sounds like Julian's old, sixty-five mustang pull up. I go to the window and peek out the blinds just in time to see them walk up to the door. I growl, watching her reaching out to touch his arm. My fist almost goes through the glass when I see Julian kiss her. No longer wanting to watch, I make my way to the couch, trying to reign in my temper. My arm covers my face. I really do need to figure out what the fuck is going on with me.

Chapter Five

Meadow

Julian pulls into an empty parking spot outside my house. The night had been fun, and though this date was fake, Julian went out of his way to make it real. He took me to dinner at this fancy restaurant with no prices on the menus and let me order whatever I wanted. We talked and he hung on my every word. Then he paid. Before the movie, we took a stroll around the lake and talked some more. Just when I thought Julian might have never been my type, tonight I might have been swayed, that's if I hadn't already given my heart to Dexter. I may have been trying to tie down Julian to be a one-woman man.

He gets out of the car and opens the door for me. "Such a gentleman," I giggle when he offers me his hand.

"I try." He winks, pulls me up, and walks me to the door.

"Thank you for doing this again." I rest my hand on Julian's shoulder.

"It's no problem. I'd do anything to help you guys, and if I can fuck with Dexter at the same time, even

69

better." He chuckles.

"I only hope it works."

"Well, considering his head was about to explode back at the office, I'd say the chances are pretty good."

"Yeah, he was pretty worked up." I grin, remembering the smoke coming out of his ears.

"I should kill him for the damn spoiler." Julian's eyes glance over my shoulder and a small smirk crosses his lips before they come landing to the corner of my mouth.

My eyes go wide at the surprise kiss. "What the hell?" I whisper and Julian flicks his finger behind me.

"He's watching the show." He steps back and my head spins around in time to see the blinds rattle, and I grin. One date and he's putty in my hands. I'm overly gleeful. I should've done this months ago.

"I should get inside then. I'll talk to you tomorrow?"

"Yep. See you, Meadow."

With one last quick hug, I find myself skipping to the front door. Picturing the jealous loon picking me up in his arms, kissing me all over and declaring his love for me finally.

Again. And sober.

Okay, I'm a bit of a spaz and using my overactive imagination, but I've always been a dreamer.

Let me have my moment.

I walk into the house and throw my purse onto the counter. The television is blaring *Jimmy Fallon* as I inch in closer to the living room. I find Dex with his arms splayed out on the back of the couch and his feet propped up on the coffee table. He doesn't look my way as I sit next to him, and my fantasy is instantly ruined.

"Hey." I nudge him grabbing his attention and

wanting the excuse to touch him.

"Oh hey, back so soon?" he says, pretending to act all surprised to see me.

I roll my eyes, tempted to beat him with the remote. "Yeah, were you waiting up?"

"Pssh, *noo*." He exaggerates the no for way too long. He's such a terrible liar, which makes me feel a little better knowing he was doing *just* that.

"Oh, really? I thought maybe you were because you're usually in bed by eleven on a work night."

"Well, Blake Lively is on Jimmy Fallon tonight, so I wanted to watch."

"We have a DVR, you know."

"She's better looking live." He gives me a lopsided grin.

"You're so full of shit." I giggle and lay my head on his shoulder.

We sit in silence as Jimmy Fallon does his Thank You Notes, but the peaceful air is broken up during the commercial break by Dexter's bitter grumble. "I'm surprised you didn't bring him inside." My head flies off him and the air around us grows tense.

"Excuse me? What kind of girl do you think I am?" I snap, and my eyes narrow, feeling a bit insulted that he would think I would just give it up.

"I don't know. I figured he would kind of push or at least try."

"He was the perfect gentleman, and I don't put out on the first date."

Just reckless one night stands with my best friend that he forgets.

"Is there going to be a second?"

Looks like there's gonna have to be because you are breaking away from the vision Dex, I muse inwardly. I've always known him to be hard-headed, but this is ridiculous.

I can practically see the steam shooting from his ears and his visions of cutting Julian up into pieces like a Looney Toon character, yet he won't open his mouth.

Could this really all be because of Wes, or is there more?

"Yes, there will be a second date." I finally answer his question. "I had fun despite the end of the movie being ruined." I bump his shoulder to lighten the mood again. There's nothing I hate more than confrontation, so I'm pleased when he loosens up and I get a laugh out of him.

"Sorry, but not really."

"Whatever, jerkface." I stand and smooth out my dress.

"Jerkface?" He snorts. "I don't think you've called me that since middle school."

"Well, since your acting like a middle schooler, the name fits. I'm going to bed. Night." I round the couch, but I don't make it far before he grabs my arm, spinning me back around. "What are you doing?"

"I wanted to tell you that you do look amazing tonight, Meadow."

My mouth pops open, taken by surprise by his words, and the sheer honesty and sweetness of them. "Thanks, Dex."

"You know, just in case he didn't tell you."

"He did, but it's nice to hear it from you too." I lean over and kiss his cheek.

He releases my arm, and I move towards the steps

for my room. I hear the television click off and seconds later Dex is next to me going upstairs.

"I saw my parents this evening and gave them the catering list. We should probably get together this week and maybe start working on our speeches."

"You mean you want me to write yours for you?" I raise my eyebrow at him.

"No, but definitely maybe make suggestions and then proofread it."

"Sure, maybe tomorrow after work?"

"Then it's a date." He winks, giving me a tap on my butt.

"A date? Then you better be buying me dinner first, sir." I huff and walk away to my room.

I'm sitting at my desk going over the final preparations for the McKinley Honorary Ball when Kayleigh Hamilton, the biggest thorn in my side, plops her nasty ass on the corner of my desk.

"Hey, M," she purrs sugary-sweet and I roll my eyes. I hate when she calls me *M*. She thinks it's cute, but it's another way for her to undermine me and show she doesn't take me seriously.

Why would she? She's always had everything handed to her. I, on the other hand, have been working my butt off since my junior year of college for Hanson Event Planners, interning and training to get to where I am now.

"Did you need something?"

She shrugs and picks up the silver frame from my desk holding a picture of Dexter and me. It's one of my favorite pictures taken at Roxann's during karaoke night. We were up on stage singing our favorite song, Queen's "You're my Best Friend." Totally cliché for us, but at least it wasn't some Journey song.

"So, when do I get to meet the famous Dexter?"

Hopefully never.

"I don't know."

"He's cute. Is he single?" Her finger traces over Dexter's face and I snatch the picture back from her and set it back on my desk.

"If there wasn't anything, I need to get back to these orders for the centerpieces, and then you need to go call the DJ and make sure he got the playlist as I told you."

"Oh, I canceled him." She shrugs again and smooths out the edges of her brown hair.

My anger flares and I'm about to pummel her to the floor.

"Excuse me? You did what? We have three days until this ball, and you canceled the DJ?" I seethe, gripping the edge of my desk.

"Yeah. I figured a live band would be much more of a hit."

"The McKinley's didn't want a live band, Kayleigh."

"They'll change their mind when they hear *The Honey Layers*. They're one of the best local bands in Sacramento."

"I don't care if you got *Maroon 5,* it's not what the

74

McKinley's wanted. They had a specific playlist. It's your job to see that you get what they wanted." My vision reddens with how angry I am. I seriously think I'm going to kill her. Snap her like a twig. Now I have another thing added to the pile of shit I have to do. I don't have time for this.

"It'll be fine, M. *The Honey Layers* said they can play most of the songs."

"Yeah most, not all," I snarl. "And the ballroom isn't set up for live entertainment." I slam my hand on my desk, sending a few of my papers flying.

"Is everything okay here, ladies?" Mr. Hanson comes into view and I'm seconds away from throwing Kayleigh under the bus when she rises off my desk and plasters on her fake ruby-red smile.

"Everything is fine, Uncle. Meadow got a live band for the benefit in three days and forgot about not having a setup. But we'll get it worked out. Right, M?"

My jaw drops to the ground, not believing she fucking did that. No, I do believe it. Now I'm going to pay for what she did.

"A live band? What happened with the DJ?" Mr. Hanson looks to me for answers. My mouth opens, ready to give up his little princess when Kayleigh steps in front of him again talking for me.

"Well, Meadow thought a live band would be a lot more beneficial and *hip*."

"What?"

Did she just say hip? I would never *say hip.*

"*Hip?*" Mr. Hanson looks at me curiously.

"No, that's *not* what I said." I stand gaping, lost for words, trying to backpedal out of this mess.

He steps away from his psycho niece and grabs my shoulders. "Meadow, you're one of my best. If you think this is the way to go, I'm trusting you. I really hope you know what you're doing. The McKinley's are one of our biggest clients."

"I know, Mr. Hanson. I have it all under control."

I'll have it under control after I throw your niece into the Sacramento River.

"Good. Now, Kayleigh can I see you in my office. I want to show you how to go over some proposals and contracts."

"Sure. Talk to you later, M." She gives me a sly smile and a mini wave before walking off, leaving me with a huge mess to clean up.

One day Meadow, you'll speak up for yourself no matter what the outcome is at the end. Or how uncomfortable it makes you.

One day.

"Ahh!" I scream, once the front door slams and I throw my purse to the counter.

"Rough day?" Dexter chuckles, sitting at the breakfast bar with his sketches spread out in front of him, a pencil behind each ear, and one in his hand.

"The fucking worst," I growl. I storm into the kitchen

and go straight for the wine.

"What happened?" He throws down his pencil and rounds the breakfast bar as I pop the cork on the Château Coutet. I need the good stuff tonight to help me chill.

"Kayleigh. She fucked me over with this huge event I've been working on." I pour myself a large glass of wine and knock it back, trying to keep my tears at bay. The stress and anger I've been holding onto all day to keep myself presentable and level headed have now boiled over. I slam the glass down and go to refill it when Dex reaches out to stop me.

"Whoa, slow down there, killer. Before you drown, tell me the rest."

My hands land on the counter and I bow my head, my hair haloing around my face. Dexter's arm is around my shoulder pulling me to his side and his lips press to the top of my head.

"She canceled the DJ, hired a live band, which wasn't what our client wanted, and then told Hanson it was all my idea with me standing right there. I froze, not knowing how to tell him that his niece was a lying bitch." I sniff, wiping the falling tears from my cheeks.

I feel like such a wuss for not being able to stand up for myself, but I also risked looking like an idiot. It's like I'm finding myself in that predicament a lot lately.

"I spent the rest of the day trying to fix it. I got the DJ back and called the McKinley's and somehow talked them into a live band for between bids, but I don't know how it's going to play out." I run my hands through my hair as I throw my head back and scream.

Dex laughs and pulls me into his chest. "Let it out, Meow."

77

I giggle. It's rare that he calls me Meow out loud these days, but it never fails to make me smile even at times like this. I grip his shirt and bury my face in his chest and yell, letting out more of my built up frustration.

"Again," Dex encourages and I scream again, to the point my throat scratches and my face heats. But it's a sweet release and I can feel some of the tension roll off my shoulders.

Finally, once I've let it all out, Dex lifts my chin, his thumb rubs the side of my cheek.

"I wonder what the next thing she might try to do. And if she takes over, hell, will I even have a job? It sucks so much because I busted my ass to get where I am in this company. And she just walks in…"

"I know. I know it's not fair. You were practically Hanson's puppet till he hired you as a senior event coordinator. But the man adores you. Maybe you should collect proof of what she's doing."

"Maybe. I feel like it would be my luck it would blow up in my face."

"Don't say that." He runs his thumb across my lips and I instinctively pucker against it. The air crackles between us and my breath hitches, but it's all ruined when my phone rings in my back pocket.

His hand falls from my face and I instantly miss the contact.

"I should get that, in case its work…" I frown not wanting to step out of his hold. He lets me go and I pull my phone from my back pocket. The name on the screen isn't who I was expecting and probably not who I need right now.

"It's Julian," I mumble. "I'll call him back."

"No, take it. We can talk later," he grunts and moves back to the breakfast bar. My phone rings one last time before going to voicemail as Dex roughly collect his papers off the table.

"Dex?" I step towards him. "What's going on with you?"

"Nothing. I'm sure you'd much rather talk to your *boyfriend,* anyway."

I pinch the bridge of my nose, knowing this is not the way I was wanting the jealousy route to go—to bitterness. "I want to talk to you."

His eyes close as he grips the mess of papers in front of him. When they open back up there's a hint of hurt and sadness that flash in them. "We can talk when you're done. Then we can go through our speeches."

"Alright." My hands slap the side of my legs as I watch him head up the stairs. I make myself another glass of wine. *A large* glass of wine and carry it to my room.

I dial Julian back and he answers after the second ring. "Hey, Meadow."

"Hey, Julian, what's going on?"

"I didn't hear from you about what happened the other night after you went inside. Did it work?" He laughs. "I was out of the office today, so I didn't get to see Dexter's reaction and there was no text from you, so I thought maybe it was good news."

"Oh, no. It was a bust. Well, not a total bust. I think he's jealous, but I'm not sure he knows why he is."

"So, does that mean we have a second date?"

"If you're sure you want to."

"Yeah, we just won't tell Dex what movie we are seeing first. When do you want to do it?"

"Can I call you tomorrow about it? Today has been rough." I sigh.

"I'm sorry. Is everything okay?" he asks sincerely, and as grateful as I am for him caring about me, the one I want to talk to is pouting in the room next to mine.

"It will be...after a couple of glasses of wine and some sleep," I say and fall back onto my bed.

"Well, this might be fake dating, but I'm here if you need to talk as friends, Meadow."

Damn, if that doesn't steal my heart. I'm tempted to vent to him, but I shake it off.

"I know, Julian. Thanks."

"Anytime, Meadow. We'll talk tomorrow then. Maybe the second time will be the charm to make Dexter's head finally blow." He laughs heartily.

"One can only hope."

Because I don't know how much more I can take before it's my heart that's the one that blows.

Chapter Six

Dexter

I never thought when I met Julian St. James out of college, thanks to my Uncle Frank, he of all people, would have the nerve to come after Meadow. Ever since I found out that he'd asked out my best friend, the question '*why her,*' has been circling through my mind. He's known her for the last three years and never shown a single interest in her besides friendship. Julian would show off his many conquests around her to the point Meadow thought he was a fuckboy. Hell, she's the one that told me Julian only hired his Secretary, Amber, so he could maybe try to fuck her. Yet, here she is going out with him.

Never thought Meadow Lexington would be this desperate.

I've been trying to shake it off the last couple days but fuck it if that hasn't worked. They don't belong together, and I stand by that.

Then, last night, to add fuel to my already tempered fire, Meadow and I were having this *moment* in the kitchen. I've always been possessive of my time with

Meadow. I've always been the one to protect her and take care of her. Then along comes Julian when I had everything under control.

What the fuck am I going to do when she doesn't need me anymore?

By the time she got off the phone with him, I no longer felt like working on our speeches. Plus, how hard will it be to tell my Aunt and Uncle how lucky they are they survived thirty-five years together, even after the tragic death of their son.

Yeah, I got it covered.

Instead, I spent the evening working out my aggression on my weight set, while Meadow drank her forty-dollar wine in two gulps watching some reality show garbage. She looked like she had been crying again and I felt like shit for not trying to comfort her over the issue at work, but she had Julian.

Now, the next morning, I have a throbbing headache, and Julian has sent me an email wanting to see me in his office to discuss a new account.

"Of course. Anything for you, Meadow…" Julian laughs and leans back in his chair. His head pops up, finally spotting me in the doorway and he waves me in. "Hey, I got to go, Dex just walked in but I'll see you tonight. Bye."

He ends the call as I plop into the tan seat in front of his mahogany desk, irritated and pissed off more than I was this morning. I cross my arms over my chest and my ankle at my knee trying to reign it in, but I'm hanging on by a proverbial thread.

"I'm glad you're here. I needed to talk to you about the Morrison account."

"What are you doing with Meadow?" I snap, not mincing words and getting down to what I need to know. What's been bugging me for days.

"What do you mean what am I doing with Meadow? I like her. What's the problem?"

"Till when?"

"What do you mean, till when?"

"Till you dump her for some other two-legged bimbo?"

"Wow, Dex." He pushes his chair back and crosses his arms, matching my position. "Is that how you think I see Meadow? As some Bimbo? Is that how you see her?"

"I didn't say that," I bark, and my fists clench at my side. How fucking dare he put words in my mouth.

"Sure sounded like it."

"Listen," I take a steady breath, "Meadow is my best friend and I see you go through women like they are disposable. She doesn't deserve that."

"That's not true. Sure, I have one night stands here and there. But I don't *use* women, Dex. You see whatever the fuck you want. Do you talk this shit about Steve? When he has Meadow help him pick up women at the bar?"

"Steve didn't ask her out," I hiss.

"And if he did, would you be this bent out?"

Yes. I would have punched Steve out a lot sooner. But Steve knows better.

"Probably."

"Fine. I dated a lot. But I figured you knew me. God. Or is it because you just want Meadow for yourself? Is that it? If you can't have her, no one can?"

"No. I just happen to know what's best for her."

He snorts and rubs his nose. "And you don't think someone like me is? Someone you've known for three years. Someone who gave you a job right out of college to help him start his own architectural firm? Who put you under his wing?"

"That's another thing. You're like four years older than her."

"Oh, now you have more excuses. And a lame one at that."

"Listen, I don't think you and Meadow are good for each other."

"Well, why don't you let me and Meadow figure that out? Right now, we're just having fun."

I cringe. Having fun? Visions of him—of his hands all over my Meadow in bed…her underneath of him…moaning…

No!

"Fun?" I snap and slam my hand on the desk. "What the fuck is that supposed to mean?"

Julian rises to his feet, his face reddens, and he slams his fist onto his desk. "You know what, Dex, I've had fucking enough, get the hell out of my office."

"Not till you tell me what you mean by fun. I have the right to know."

"Actually, you don't. If Meadow wants to tell you, she will. But as for right now, what goes on between Meadow and me stays between Meadow and me. Now leave my office before I do something I might regret."

"Like what?" I challenge the motherfucker. He wouldn't do anything.

"Like fire your ass for being insubordinate."

"You wouldn't."

"Try me right now," he hisses. "I've let it go up to this point because I get you love Meadow and for some reason, you can't admit you're acting more like a jealous asshole than maybe her friend. And you're also forgetting that you're my employee. You're seconds the fuck away from knocking me out. Now I want you out of my face and I'll email you about the Morrison account."

I get to the door and stop leaning my head on the frame. "Jules," I mutter.

"What?"

I turn back to him watching him shuffle through the papers, no longer seeming affected by the fight. "Me and Meadow have just been through hell and back. It's not you…"

It is you—but I won't say any more on that.

"I know man. I'm not going to hurt her. But maybe you need to look in the mirror and see what it is that you want."

"Right." I close my eyes and know I need to separate my work and personal life before everything blows up in my face. "I'm sorry. I won't...can we just…" I struggle with the words not wanting to say them, "…pretend I wasn't being a dick moments ago?"

He looks back up at me, unexpectedly, and rolls his eyes. "Fine. Sit down."

The rest of the meeting goes off without a hitch as we discuss the Morrison contract. I'll give it to Julian; he always had a way of brushing shit off and moving on. While I, on the other hand, might have been still stewing, wondering if I could set him up to maybe look like he's screwing around on Meadow.

Not that I would, I still have some morals, but it

made the meeting easier and I figured the thought was better than breaking his face.

When I make it back to my office, I grab my phone and text Meadow, seeing if I convince her to hang out with me tonight.

Wanna hang out tonight?
We didn't finish those speeches
and I got you a brand new bottle
of Château Coutet 2013 with
your name on it.
Since you drank the other
one in under a minute.

I haven't got it *yet*. But I will after my lunch break.

Meow: Awww Thank you.
You didn't have to do that though.
I would have been fine with some
Barefoot. And I can't tonight.
I already made plans.
Can we maybe hang out tomorrow?

Yeah, tomorrow.

Meow: You're not mad,
are you?

Of course not.
I have a lot to do anyways.
I'll probably just work late instead.

Meow: Alright.
4Evr&evr you know that right?

I sigh and rake my hands through my hair wondering why she would ever question that.

Forever and Ever.
No doubt.

I, Dexter Greene, am alone on a Friday night. It's fucking pathetic. I wonder if I should take Steve's advice and go out and pick up a random girl and fuck her to forget this sad state.

Hey, wanna grab some
beers at Mike's Tavern?

Steve: Shit Man, I actually have
a date with that hottie
waitress from the other day.

What the fuck? When did Steve start *dating?* First, Julian takes my girl to make relationship strides, and now Steve is showing off?

Great.

~~Didn't think you bought them dinner first.~~

I backspace and delete that. I've acted like a dick enough today to my friends and don't know how Steve would take that. Instead, I take the simple route.

Oh, awesome man.
Have fun.

> *Steve: Shit you know I will.*
> *If you want, I can see*
> *if she has a friend?*

My finger hovers over the Y key, knowing it's probably what I need to get rid of whatever is bugging me with Meadow. But the thought leaves an uneasy feeling in my stomach and I pass.

No. I'm good.
I'll see you later, man.

I throw my phone to my bed, then myself. I debate calling Mel to see if she wants to hang out, but more than likely she'll just rag on me.

Maybe Julian is right, and I need to figure out what the fuck is going on with me.

I rest my hands under my head and look to the ceiling, my mind drifting to the first night we moved into this house.

We had recently graduated from college. Julian had

hired me right on as a junior architect, Meadow had gotten a full-time position at Hanson Event Planners, and along with some financial help from our parents, we were able to buy this house. We had bought some new bedroom furniture and, well, mine arrived on time and Meadow's didn't. So, I let her sleep in my bed that night.

Meadow comes bouncing into my bed in a pair of blue flannel pajama pants and an oversized blue t-shirt. In her arms is her dog, Pickles.

"I still can't believe they forgot my furniture." She rolls her eyes and sits the imitation Taco Bell Dog onto my bed on my left. The little bastard nips at my leg and I shove him away. He then makes himself comfortable on an extra pillow by my feet. I'm sure he's waiting for me to sleep to make his next attack.

Out of all the dogs at the pound, I picked the one that liked the taste of my blood.

"Well, hopefully, they'll have it right tomorrow or I'll be getting your money back."

She pulls back the covers and scoots herself into my side, resting her head in the crook of my shoulder.

"Do you have to sleep right on top of me?" I groan, but I don't mind.

"Yeah. You're so warm, and it'll only be till I fall asleep. You know I'll roll over and my feet will be in your ribs in no time."

I chuckle, having no doubt about that. The girl wiggles like crazy in her sleep.

"Dex?"

"Yeah?"

"It's a good thing you don't have a girlfriend right

now."

"Why is that?" She lifts her leg, and her bent knee runs along my semi-erect crotch. My hands fly down and push her away. "I can't help that."

"Oh yeah?"

"Meadow!" I grit between my teeth, narrowing my eyes. What does she expect? I've been like this for as long as I remember when she would sleep in my bed. Sometimes I could control it, other times, especially in the morning, well, forget it. My dick has a mind of its own and there's no denying that Meadow is sorta attractive, and my dick might be a little attracted.

"What? I'm only messing with you." She falls into a fit of giggles, rolling away from me. It gives me a chance to grab a free pillow and place it over my junk.

"I'll make you sleep on the floor if you don't cut that shit out."

"No, I'm good. Thanks."

"But I really should make the dog."

Pickles growls at me, baring his little teeth.

"No, he loves you." She scratches under his chin, making him settle.

"He hates me."

"All lies. You saved his little dog life from the shelter. You need to be nicer. He thinks it's like a game to hate you, but I saw him licking your face yesterday."

"That was him trying to eat my face." Okay, I do like the little shit of a dog. I have to bribe him with food for him to be nice to me. The second that dog was in Meadow's arms he took over my job as her best friend and protector. The thing might be five pounds, but it'll rip through your skin.

"No, he wasn't. They were kisses for feeding him your bacon." She giggles, cuddling back into my side. *"Do you think the people we marry will understand our best friend time?"* Meadow ponders randomly, rubbing her hand up my chest.

"If you mean lying in bed like this together, and you rubbing on my crotch...probably not," I joke and she smacks me. Pickle stands on his little legs, barking at her, coming to my defense of her attack.

"Wow, dog. You finally have my *back?"* I pet the top of his head and he settles back down in his spot.

"Told you he loves you...and I didn't mean like that. Like for twenty-something years we've seen each other every day. If we start like getting serious with someone, you know that will change, unless they understand because they are super awesome. Or we grow apart."

"Well, we will have to find some people that are super awesome."

She frowns. *"I doubt I could find anyone else like Wes, unless it's..."* she pauses and looks down at her hand laying on my chest, *"you."* The word comes out above a whisper, but I hear it.

"Let's not worry about that now and get some sleep. The rest of our stuff should be in tomorrow."

"It better be. Or the delivery guy is going to have my foot up his ass."

"I love you, Meadow."

"Love you too, Dex. Forever and Ever."

I wake suddenly, blinking as I adjust to the light from my lamp I never turned off. Looking at my watch it reads three a.m. and I realize I must've passed out daydreaming about the past.

With the urge to pee, I roll out of bed to relieve myself. Once I'm done, I wonder if Meadow is home and decide to go check on her. When I get to the hallway, I find the house dark and quiet, which tells me she's home because I'm pretty sure I left all the downstairs lights on.

When I get to her door, I put my ear against it and when I hear nothing, I crack the door open. I brace myself, worried about what I might find, but I need to know that she's home—and I hope alone.

I can make out her soft breathing as I step into her room. The moonlight shines in from her picture window and illuminates over her bed, revealing that she's indeed alone.

"Thank god," I breathe.

For a moment, I stand and watch her sleep. This was something I used to do for hours after Wes died, after she would finally cry herself to sleep. I found myself unable to sleep from the guilt, so I would watch her, counting her breaths, thankful I still had her. Though it had been thanks to me I cost her everything. If she ever knew what I did that night Wes died, she would hate me forever.

The sheets crinkle as Meadow turns over, and she makes a little moan in her sleep. The sound makes my dick hard in an instant and I fucking curse at it for it always reacting to her at the wrong fucking time. I back out of her room, knowing I'll have to take care of *this* before I get back to sleep tonight.

Yeah, I have a lot to fucking think about.

Too bad everything leads to me still never being able to have her.

Chapter Seven

Dexter

"Dexter," Meadow's voice whispers in my ear waking me from a heavy sleep.

"Meadow?" I breathe, my eyes peel open to see her smiling face hovering above me. "What are you doing?"

"What does it look like I'm doing?" she giggles, and she plants a kiss to my lips, then across my cheek to my neck. "This is what you want, isn't it? What you keep thinking about doing to me when you masturbate every night?"

Her hand traces down my chest as she sits up on my hips exposing her glorious, naked body to me. How have I never noticed how sexy she's become? How perfect and round her breasts are, or how soft her skin is? Or how overall perfect she is?

"Fuck me, Dex. Make me yours."

"We shouldn't." The words leave my lips as I grab her hips and flip her over on the mattress. She squeals, her hand gripping into my hair and her legs wrap around my back.

95

"We shouldn't, huh?" Her eyebrow quirks, with a cheeky grin.

"No, but seeing as were both naked and you're here…" Her beautiful green eyes light up and she bites the corner of her lip. Damn, that's fucking sexy. Why haven't I noticed how hot *that* is before*? "Fuck."*

I press my lips to hers, and slip my tongue between them, needing to taste her.

She moans underneath me, her wet core wiggling against the tip of my dick. "Tell me how much you want this."

"I want you so bad." Her hips thrust into me eagerly and she pulls my head back down to kiss me.

Slowly, I sink into her, and her warmth wraps around my dick. It's heaven. A tight, velvety heaven.

"Oh, Dexter…Dexter…" she whispers my name. Then it's followed by a light banging noise. It happens again and when I open my eyes, Meadow is gone and I'm on my back.

The sun is pouring into my window and as I look around the room, I realize it has all been a fucking dream.

"Dexter? You awake yet?" Meadow's voice echoes through the door and the handle jiggles.

"Fuck!" I'm instantly alert and panicked grabbing for the sheets to cover my hard-on. "Yeah?"

"Did you still want to go for that hike and work on our speeches?"

"One second," I yell and scramble off the bed to find a pair of my basketball shorts. I slip them on and make my way to my door. Opening it a crack, I hide my bottom half behind it, giving her a weak smile.

"You okay?" she giggles at me which does nothing

to help the granite hard dick I'm sporting.

Neither do the tight leggings and sports bra she's wearing. God, she would kill me and my dick on this hike today.

"No. Actually, I'm not feeling all that great."

"Oh, you do look a little flushed." She reaches out to touch my face and I back away. Her face falls along with her hand. "Okay then, I'll let you rest. It looks like you knocked out early too. You forgot to turn the lights off."

"Yeah, I passed out the second I laid down."

"Can I get you anything?"

Yeah, out of my room, so I can finish what my dream didn't. Then figure out what the fuck is going on with me lately with all these feelings *and learn how to control them.*

"No. I'm good. Thanks."

"Alright, if you're sure. Maybe if you feel better later, we can hang out?" she offers, biting the corner of her lip. Fuck, if that doesn't make me want to reach out and kiss her…*and* make my dick harder.

Damn it. Dex, get her out of here.

"Yes, later." I'm seconds from closing the door in her face when she gives me another confused wide-eyed look before walking away.

Closing the door, I lock it and lose my shorts before settling back into my bed. Fisting my cock, I close my eyes and think of her.

The only place I'll ever be able to have her.

I spend half the morning hiding out in my room, not sure how to look Meadow in the eye. It isn't only because every time I think of her my dick twitches. It's the mountain-sized pile of guilt that turns my stomach every single time. Friends don't masturbate and have sex dreams about their friends. No matter how close they are. Especially friends whose hearts they don't deserve and don't belong to them.

My conclusion to all this nonsense is I need to get laid. It's been a year. Steve and Randy are right; I only have excuses as to why I'm not dating or picking up women.

What the hell am I waiting for?

It's just the urge hasn't *been* there *till* I think of Meadow.

I have no idea what I'm going to do, but I know I can no longer avoid her.

By late afternoon, I make the escape from my room to find Meadow in the living room working away. She has a huge event tomorrow she claims she's still not ready for, thanks to the mess her coworker made. Once she finishes with that, we have a late lunch, forget about the speeches and watch some trash TV instead.

Now, she's skipping into my room after I've finished taking a shower.

I need to get better about locking my door.
But then she'll know something is up.
At least I have my pants on.

"We're all going to Roxann's. Do you wanna come?" Meadow flops on my bed, wearing a pair of tight-fitting jeans and a low-cut gray tank top. Her auburn hair flies out around my pillow making her look like an angel.

"Who's all?" I question throwing my favorite Nine Inch Nails shirt over my head.

She props herself on her elbows and looks at me with her trademark innocent grin. Which is technically anything but…because it usually means she's up to something.

"Me, Mel, Steph, Steve, Randy, Sara..." She pauses and bites her lip.

I roll my eyes, now knowing what her little smile is all about; her damn new boyfriend. She's worried about me behaving, which tells me Julian has probably told her all about my spectacle in his office yesterday.

Just fucking great.

"And Julian, right?"

"Yeah. The usual. It's karaoke night. And they got an updated song list from this generation now. I bet we could totally kill some *Chainsmokers* and *Bruno Mars*." She rolls off my bed and I'm tempted to push her back down and reenact my dream.

My dick is jerking in my jeans, telling me to do it, and I really wish it wouldn't. The bastard has always had different views when it came to her anyway. *He* wouldn't mind me losing all my self control and diving right into her.

But you *can't have her, Dex. She's not yours! She*

will never be yours. Get it through your head.

Control yourself.

"Would I really have a choice anyways?"

"Not really, since I know you're feeling better. Now finish getting ready. I ordered us a uber. It should be here in ten minutes."

Meadow and I walk into Roxann's where we are greeted by someone butchering Neil Diamond's "Sweet Caroline."

"Is there nothing better than the sound of someone killing the classics?" Meadow mutters beside me with a giggle.

"Yeah. Someone not *murdering* them. Come on." I take her hand and lead her to the large round table where our friends and *Julian* are gathered around.

Meadow tugs on my arm, grabbing my attention before we make it too far, and I look down at her narrowing eyes. "Be nice."

"I don't know what you're talking about." I smirk, but my lip twitches, calling out my lie.

"He's your friend, and no matter what, that comes first. Can we please have fun tonight?" Her slit eyes go doe-like and there's no way I can deny her. So for tonight, I can put the asshole aside for her.

"Of course, Meow."

"You've been calling me that a lot more lately. I like it." She kisses my cheek and then goes bouncing off towards the table.

I touch my cheek as I follow behind her. I didn't even realize I was calling her that intentionally, but if she likes it, who am I to deny her?

"Good, you're both finally here," Steph says and throws her arm around Meadow. "I got us all shots. Then us girls are going to sing "Spice Up Your Life.""

"Spice Girls? Right out the gate, Steph? Really? Better make it two shots." Meadow puts her hand up to grab the attention of one of the bartenders.

"Wait. I thought we came here tonight to try the new songs." Steve grabs his shot and Mel slaps his hand telling him not yet. "Damn lady, chill."

"We will. I promise you'll get to rock some Twenty One Pilots. *After* we rock some old school up in this bitch." Steph pats his back reassuring him and he rolls his eyes. "Now let's toast to a good night."

We all pick up the kamikaze shots and click them together before throwing them back.

The night starts off smoothly with the girls bringing down the house with their rendition of Spice Girls. The four of them are always house favorites when they get on stage together or separate. Meadow especially. She has a voice like an angel.

Well, till she has a couple of shots then she gets giggly and squeaky on purpose.

No matter what I tried to do, I found myself drawn to Meadow all night. Everywhere she went, my eyes followed. I watched how she and Julian interacted, and I found myself taking a shot every time his arm ended up around her shoulder.

At one point, Steve had told me some blonde with a banging body had been all over me and I didn't even acknowledge her existence. There wasn't enough liquor in the place to help wipe my mind of everything I was thinking.

"You've been watching her all night," Mel says, coming to sit beside me at the bar top with her fruity martini.

"What? Who?" I shake my head, drawing my attention away from Meadow's ass that's bent over a few tables in front of us.

"Don't play dumb with me, pretty boy. Meadow."

"No. I haven't."

"You have. And more than usual."

I roll my eyes and relent. There's no getting past the master detective in Mel. "I'm making sure she's okay. She's knocking back the Cuervo more than usual. I know work has been stressing her out."

"Right." She squints at me, taking a sip of her pink martini.

"Don't look at me like that, Mel."

"Like what?" she says innocently with a squeak of her voice and blinky eyes.

"I know what you want to say. It's all I've been hearing from everyone lately—even my own mother. But I wish everyone would give it a rest. There are things that you all don't understand and will never understand when it comes to Meadow and me."

"Try me."

"No."

"Does it have something to do with Wesley?"

"Mel, I love you. You're like this annoying little sister."

"Aww. I try to be." She puts her hand over her heart and flutters her eyes. I shake my head knowing she's proved my point.

"But I'm not explaining this to you. Especially not here, and especially not while Randy and Sara sing "Endless Love" off-key in the background."

"Fine, you make a fair point. Plus, I think I have my answer anyways." She winks, grabbing her martini, and steps away.

Seconds later, Meadow is coming at me with a large smile on her face. Her cheeks and chest are flushed, and her once neat hair is now a wild mess, a clear sign that she's wasted.

"DEX!" Meadow collapses onto my chest and puts her arms around my neck. "We need to sing our song."

"We do, huh?"

"We do," she says in a sing-song voice. "Or we can do something new. Oh, we can totally try that Lady Gaga and Bradley Cooper song."

"That song always makes you cry." I laugh.

"Does not." I narrow my eyes at her to say yeah right. I found her the other day wiping her eyes to some YouTube video of them singing it. "Fine. We can stick to old faithful then."

"Sure you don't want to ask…" She slams her forefingers to my lips, meshing them together before I can say Julian's name.

"Don't say it or I'm gonna kick your butt." She moves my lips around and giggles making me question if I missed counted the number of drinks she's had tonight.

I grab her wrist and remove her hand from my mouth. "Alright, goof, I think it's time to get you home."

"Home?" She pouts. "But we need to *sinnng.*"

"No, because you have had enough."

"Then I'll stop drinking, *Dad.* Geez, I'm talking about singing." She juts her bottom lip out more, knowing I'm not going to say no to her.

"Fine, one song." I brush my thumb along her soft pouting lip, pushing it back in. "Then I'm taking you home."

Her eyes dance mischievously and her tongue darts out of her mouth wetting her lips. Those satin lips that I can now picture around my dick. I shift uncomfortably in my seat. *Fuck.* "What are you gonna do to me when you get me home, Dex? Spank me?"

"Damn it, Meadow."

"What? You're the one who made it sound dirty." She falls into a fit of giggles and I pinch the bridge of my nose, now stressed the fuck out.

I need to get away from her. Now.

Picking up my beer, I step around her to go to the bar to tell Julian I'm taking her ass home. I don't get far when she grabs my arm and pulls me back. "Dex, I was playing around."

"Listen, Meadow, I'm tired. I want to go home. You can either come with me or stay with Julian. Up to you."

"I'll come with you," she says quickly, which instantly relaxes me. "Let's go say bye first. But you owe me a song next time."

"Deal."

We get into the house and her shoes go flying at the door before I turn on the light. "Oh, so much better," she moans and stumbles her way to the couch. She falls into the cushions, throwing her now bare feet on the coffee table.

I join her, kicking off my own shoes, and slide in next to her on the couch. "How many of those tequila shots did you take tonight?" I joke nudging her as her head falls to my shoulder.

"Not enough." She sighs heavily and rubs her hand down my jeaned legs. When she sighs again, this time more dramatically, I know something is on her mind.

"What's wrong?"

"Do you love me, Dex?"

Wait. What?

Not the question I saw coming.

"You know I do, Meadow. What makes you think I don't?"

She sits up, shifting to look me dead in the eye. "No Dex, I wanna know if you can love, *love* me! Because I do. I *love* you."

My eyes close, not sure how to reply to her. She *loves* me?

She's drunk and doesn't know what *she's talking about.*

"I can be great you know," she slurs, shoving her finger in my chest.

"You are great, Meadow. You're my favorite person."

"Then why am I not enough for you? Why can't you be with me?" Her voice cracks, and tears well in the corner of her eyes.

"Meadow." I don't know what to say, so I do the only thing I do know, and I take her in my arms. She wraps her arms around my waist and rests her cheek to my chest.

"Why can't you love me more than just a friend. Wes did. We were happy."

My eyes closed pained at the sound of his name. "It's not like that."

God, it's anything, but.

"Then what is it like? Because I know you *do*, but you're doing everything in your power not to. Why don't you want me, Dex? Why?" she cries, burying her head further into my chest, letting her tears soak my shirt.

I brush her hair back, trying to process the words I want to say. There's so much to say and my heart is heavy, knowing it can never be. The word 'why' is softy muttered again in my chest before I feel her body go limp in my arms.

"Meadow?" Lifting her chin, I find her eyes closed and her breathing even. "Meadow? Really?" I chuckle knowing only this girl could pass out in the middle of a conversation slash argument. Or whatever the hell this was.

I carry her to her room, lay her down in her bed, and sit beside her. As she snores softly, I watch her chest rise and fall. I brush her hair back, wishing it could all be simple.

"I want to love you, Meadow, I really do, but I can't. I don't deserve you. If it weren't for me, you would be with Wes now. You deserve someone that won't fuck up your life because they were being selfish. Or a guy that ties you to trees when your eleven or changes out your hair dye for bright orange before homecoming." I chuckle knowing I'm going down memory lane with a comatose body. Bending down, I kiss her lips and relish for a second in how soft they are. She moans and her eyes flutter open as I break away. I freak out, feeling busted for the move, but a small smile creases her lips before they quickly shut again.

"Meadow? You awake there?" Silence. "Meadow?" Still nothing and I cover her up with her comforter. "No matter what, I'll love you forever and ever." I brush my finger down her face and rise to my feet. With one last glance at her, I make a final silent statement; that even though I'll never be her happy ending, I'll do everything I can to make sure she's happy and that one day she ends up with the right person…

But I know one thing: that person isn't Julian.

"Good morning, sunshine." I chuckle, as the disaster of my best friend walks into the kitchen. Her hair is a rat's nest on top of her head, her eyes have dark circles under them, and she's still wearing the clothes she wore to the bar last night. But in a way, she's still never looked better. "Coffee?"

"Please," she begs, plopping down on the stool at the breakfast bar. "And the whole bottle of aspirin if you have it." Her head falls to the table with a loud groan.

I pour her a cup of coffee and slide it in front of her slumped over body. "Here you go, princess. You want any food?"

Her head pops up and she takes the mug from me putting it to her lips. "No, I want to die. And I have the McKinley Ball this afternoon. Hell, I don't even know how I got to bed."

"I put you there. I practically had to carry you home. Then you passed out when we were talking on the couch. I put you to bed afterward."

"Ugh." Her body slides back to the bar like jello. "I don't remember anything past singing Anne-Marie's '2002' and Sara making me take that Mind Eraser."

I smirk. "It might literally have been just that."

Inside I'm sighing in relief she doesn't remember our conversation on the couch. The last thing I want to do is hurt her or ruin our friendship because I can't give her what she wants.

Yet, why does it hurt?

"What are you talking about?" Her eyes peek from her folded arms.

"Oh, nothing, Meow." I wave off, with a light chuckle. I need her off the topic before she starts asking too many questions and breaks me down.

"Meow?" Her eyebrow raises. "Okay, now I know

something is up."

Shit. That was dumb, Dexter.

"Nothing is up. Only that if you can't remember past that, you have a lot of blank space that was voided. That's all." I cross my fingers at my side that she buys it and lets it go.

"I didn't do anything stupid, did I?"

"Nope." I give her my best innocent smile, because it wasn't *stupid*.

Only that you confessed a deep dark secret.

"Promise?"

"I promise."

Her body melts back to the breakfast bar, with an exaggerated moan. "I don't believe you, but I'm not in the mood to argue with you."

Thank god for a small victory.

Chapter Eight

Dexter

Meadow got back from her event late and I didn't see her before I passed out for the evening. I knew I couldn't have her, but more than ever I wanted to be in her presence. Talk to her, touch her—*hold her*. More than what we already do. That in itself is frightening.

What we talked about the night before, or what we had drunk talked about, had been forgotten from Meadow's memory but it still bounced around in mine.

Meadow is in love with me.

It had been a drunk confession, and I wondered why she hasn't told me the words sober. But then again, I knew why. If she had been sober and aware of the words I said, the outcome could be detrimental to our friendship.

I can't imagine what person can still pretend everything is okay after their feelings were turned down.

Not saying we couldn't overcome the storm, but it was a risk. Plus, maybe she didn't mean *those* words, considering she was still dating Julian.

The whole thing is confusing as fuck, and I don't

know what to do with it all. It's messing with me. And even though I can't have her, I know Julian isn't the right guy. Sure, most of my reasons are purely selfish as to why he can't be with her, but fuck if I care. I stand by it and will see they aren't together much longer.

Seeing them together is killing me.

That's what brings me to Meadow's work today. I'm surprising her for lunch, in hopes to talk to her out of dating him. Again.

When I enter Meadow's office, I find it empty with her computer closed. I pull out my phone to text her and find out where she is when someone taps me on the shoulder. I turn around and I'm met by a woman with a bright, ruby-red smile and flowing brown hair.

"You look a little lost. Can I help you?" she says sweetly, and inches in closer to my personal space.

"I was looking for Meadow. Do you know where she is?"

"You're Dexter, right?" She points her long-manicured nail at me, giving me a flirty laugh.

"That's me."

"Oh my god. I've heard so much about you. I'm Kayleigh." She holds out her hand, "M, talks about you *all* the time."

M?

I've given Meadow some crazy nicknames over the years but there's no way in hell that she would let that one fly. I take her hand and shake it, giving her a nod. "Yeah? Well um...do you know where she is?"

"She had a meeting with some guy this afternoon for lunch."

"A guy?" I clear my throat. "Was his name Julian, by

chance?"

"I think so." She shrugs and smooths out the strands at the bottom of her hair.

My blood boils because I should have known something was up when Jules ran out of the office suddenly claiming he needed to meet some 'special client.' Now I feel like an idiot thinking I could surprise my best friend for lunch when her boyfriend had already beat me to it.

"Well, thanks. I should be going." I point my thumb over my shoulder at the door and step back towards it.

"Hey, if you want…" She reaches out and touches my arm, "maybe me and you could grab some lunch. I know this cute little diner down the road, not far from here. I mean, you did come all this way."

"I don't know."

"Come on. I don't bite." She winks and runs her hand along my shoulder. "You still have to eat. What do you say?"

I rub my neck and shift on my feet. This is trouble. It will be my head if I go, but I haven't been thinking straight lately. Though it's not like Meadow isn't with him, not caring about *my* feelings. And it's only lunch. *I do have to eat.* "Sure. Why not."

We head down to a little diner across the street and settle into the vinyl booth. I pick up a menu and flip through the couple of pages trying to pay more attention to it then the girl who is busy playing with her hair across from me. I have no idea what to say to this girl, considering all I know about her is how much Meadow despises her. It's awkward. After the waitress comes by and takes our order, I drum my fingers on the table, playing a rendition of Van Halen's "Hot for Teacher," to kill the time till the food comes.

This was a bad idea.

"Hey," Kayleigh covers my hand with hers stopping me mid-chorus and reminding me where I am, "so what is that you do? I don't think M ever told me?"

"I thought she talked about me a lot?"

Her eyes widen, then she giggles uncomfortably. I'm unsure what she's uncomfortable about, but I have a feeling it's because all the conversations were overheard and not told to her. "She does. It's just she never mentioned what you did. It was mainly other stuff. Like what you did on weekends and stuff."

"I'm an architect at SJD Designs."

"An architect. Wow, that's amazing!" Her hazel eyes light up. "Is that what you always wanted to do?"

"It is. I've always loved drawing and building since I was little. I designed my childhood treehouse for me, Meadow, and my cousin, Wes." I chuckle at the memory. I was only seven, but I knew then I wanted to be a designer of houses more than the one to build them.

"I think it's crazy that you guys have known each other for so long and are still so close. I drifted apart from most everyone I grew up with. Even the ones from high school." She picks up her water that the waitress brought us a few minutes ago and takes a sip.

"I got lucky." I grin. Even with everything happening between us now, there's not a day that goes by that I couldn't be more grateful that Meadow is in my life.

"Meadow probably doesn't think I like her, does she?"

Her question catches me off guard and I clear my

throat.

"You don't have to answer that." She waves her hands, appearing anxious to backtrack. "I know you're her best friend. I want you to know that I do admire her and look up to her. My uncle thinks she's the star at her job." She sighs and her eyes drift to the large open window beside us. "I feel awful about what happened the other day." Her hands play with the bottom of her hair, *again,* and she looks back over at me with a large pouty frown. "You see, the other day we had a misunderstanding with a DJ. I didn't mean to upset her so much. I thought I was doing the right thing. A step out of her book."

"Listen, Kayleigh," I fall back in the booth and loosen my tie that suddenly feels very tight around my neck, "this isn't any of my business. You should take it up with Meadow. She's probably one of the most understanding people I know."

"I did try. At the ball. She avoided me big time. She got the DJ back and thank goodness everything worked out the way it was supposed to. I'd hoped maybe you had some advice on how to approach her. It's why I asked you to lunch when I saw you. I was hoping to get some information out of you on how to talk to her."

So, I'm just a pawn. Great.

"Just give her time. That's all I can say. I'm sure by your next event everything will work itself out."

"You're right. Thanks, Dex." She tucks her hair behind her ear and smiles.

We finish up our lunch and I walk her back to her office. I figure maybe I can still catch Meadow before I head back to work, though I have no idea what I will say to her. Or what she will say if she knows I was out with

Kayleigh.

Unless I lie.

Who am I kidding? Meadow can see me lying a mile away.

"Thanks for joining me," Kayleigh says as I open the large glass door for her to the office building.

"You're welcome, Kayleigh. Thanks for the invite."

"We should totally do it again." She grabs my hand and pulls me into a hug. Over her shoulder I spot Meadow, talking to Ariel, the receptionist, holding a pile of papers.

"Yeah, possibly," I mumble and pull away, but it's not quick enough and Meadow makes eye contact with me. She continues to talk to Ariel who is typing on the computer in front of her, but her green eyes darken angrily. I instantly know I'm a dead man when she gets a hold of me.

"Sounds great. I should get back." Kayleigh gives me a little wave that I catch out of the corner of my eye since I haven't unlocked my sights from Meadow. Seeing the hurt and anger flare in her eyes, I feel like shit, but at the same time, the asshole in me feels satisfied I got to her. Perhaps now she'll know how I've been feeling about her and Julian.

I step towards her, but she shakes her head, and I stop. Her jaw is tense, and she points to the front door silently asking me to leave.

Rather than ask to be killed *now,* I turn around and make my escape.

The front door slams and I'm off the couch, ready for the fight I've been preparing for all day. I turn to see Meadow throw her purse to the ground and I give her a cheeky smile. In return she snarls at me, I mean legit snarls, like a tiger seconds from clawing my eyes out.

"What the fuck were you doing with Kayleigh this afternoon?"

"We had lunch," I say calmly, and I don't think I've ever seen her face turn red so fast. I worry she might explode.

"You had lunch with Kayleigh? Are you fucking serious?" Meadow bellows, throwing her clunky bracelet to the counter, making a loud thud. Next, her high heels come flying off and they whiz past my face, nearly hitting me. I'm pretty sure the intent was to make direct contact.

"Yeah, so what?" I shrug, acting like I don't care that she didn't just try to take my eye out with her heel. "You were out with Julian and I was hungry."

"What are you talking about? I wasn't out with Julian. I had lunch with a client."

"That's not what Kayleigh said."

"Excuse me?" she scoffs. "Kayleigh doesn't know shit."

"You don't have to lie to me, *M.*" Fire ignites in her eyes and her fists clench at her sides. Yeah, I've pissed her off more, but I don't care at this moment. I'm already on a roll and there's no stopping me now. "Julian went out with a surprise client this afternoon too. I get it, you two don't want to rub it in my face anymore or whatever. You don't have to lie about it though. It's fine."

"It's not fine, Dexter. You went out with Kayleigh. Someone who I consider right now as my mortal enemy. Haven't you been listening to anything I say?"

"She isn't all that bad." I flick a piece of invisible lint off my pants.

"She's a fucking bitch!" Meadow screeches, loud enough it makes my ears ring. Her face reddens further as she moves in closer to me. "I've told you how much I hate her. And you have the nerve to take her out to lunch?"

"She's really not." Kayleigh was a little annoying, but overall, she wasn't that bad. "Maybe you haven't given her a chance. I get she's pissed you off, but I believe she wants to try to get to know you. She said she admires you and says she was sorry."

"Oh my god, Dex. You can't *actually* believe that."

"I do. She said at the ball you avoided her when she tried to apologize."

"I can't believe I'm hearing this," she utters in disbelief, looking around the room at anywhere but me. "She didn't try to apologize! What she *did* was once again tried to get my DJ to leave when he arrived. Then fucked with my servers so they were confused and late."

"Come on. I doubt that."

"You're siding with her?" she sneers, inching closer to my face. The heat radiating off her is enough to melt me and everything around us, but I don't back down.

"I didn't say that!"

"You know what? This is all beside the point, Dex. I can't believe all this. So, what are you two, dating now?"

"For one, it was just lunch. And I might have asked her to dinner," I lie and I'm not even sure where that came from, but I go with it. At this point, it's too late to wipe away the shell-shocked jaw drop on Meadow's face. "Plus, why does it matter? It's not like you stopped dating Julian after I asked you not to."

"Oh my god. Julian is nothing like Kayleigh. Also, I don't remember you ever asking me *not* to date him." Meadow grips the top of her hair and yanks at it. "Julian is at least your friend. He's never backstabbed you."

"He did when he went out with you," I yell, stabbing my finger at her. She stares at me for a second and shakes her head. That's when I see the tears welling in the corners of her eyes. The anger that was once there is replaced by a trembling chin of defeat.

"You know what? I'm done. You can talk to me when you get your head out of your ass. For now, stay the hell away from me."

The air in the house has shifted this last week. Meadow's cold shoulder has turned our once warm house into the freakin' arctic. Not even those days where she was acting like a demon would compare to how she's acting now. In fact, I would take those days back in a heartbeat.

It was a mistake going to lunch with Kayleigh and then lying about asking her for dinner. Now I'm paying for it. Never in the twenty-four years we've known each other have we had a fight like this, where neither one of us is willing to be the first to back down or just get over it. I do regret some of the things I said to her. Then again, she hasn't listened to me once about how I felt about Julian.

And she told me she loved me, and she still proceeds to go out with him.

Do I even matter to her?

I only wanted her to feel for a second what I was going to through. Maybe Kayleigh wasn't the right choice, but it's not like I could ask Mel or Steph. Who else is going to get under Meadow's skin?

I twirl my keys on my finger waiting for my little ice-princess to come downstairs so we can drive to meet my parents to finish setting up everything for Wes' parents' anniversary party. It's only going to take thirty seconds for one of our mothers to pick up on the tension between us so it's going to make for an interesting lunch.

"Are you coming?" I yell up the stairs getting annoyed now. I want to get this over with.

Finally, I hear her bedroom door slam and she's coming down the stairs in a pink flowery sundress. She looks amazing, besides the angry scowl on her face.

"I told you I would meet you there." She charges past me and picks up her purse off the counter. She digs through it and pulls out her keys.

"It's just as easy to go together."

"It is, but I prefer to drive myself. I might meet up with Mel and Steph afterward."

"Not Julian?" I hiss his name and her hands ball into fists so tight at her sides I worry the keys might bruise her hands.

"You know if you would get your head out of your ass and maybe look around you for once, you could see what's really going on. But for whatever reason, you'd rather be an asshole and hurt me."

"Me? I think that's where you have it all wrong, *sister.*"

Her green eyes darken and her jaw ticks before she turns on her heel charging for the front door. She flings it open and slams it right behind her.

Great.

Taking a deep breath, I go to catch up with her, but the second I'm out the door she's already peeling out of the driveway. I'm in my truck and screeching out of my spot to follow after her. When she turns at the off ramp of the highway, she picks up speed and my anger boils when I realize she's now going twenty over the speed limit. Does she not give a shit about her safety? Does she not remember how Wes died?

My hand slams into the dashboard as the memory of that night seeps into my mind. The night that could have been prevented if it wasn't for me.

The three of us are piled in the front of Wes' pickup truck. Meadow is passed out with her head on my shoulder. Wes picked Meadow and me up from a party up in the Valley, a party he didn't want me to take his girlfriend to because we would be drinking—and it was 'irresponsible' or some bullshit since he had to work and couldn't be with us. It was the first huge party of the summer and I wanted to hang out with Meadow. I don't need his permission to do so! It's like Wes had turned some power play on my friendship just because they're dating. I get it, he loves her. But she's still my best friend and I wanted to drink and party with her. So, I took her.

The only problem was when the party ended, we were left without a ride. No cab was willing to come and get us that far and none of our friends were sober enough to drive us home. So I called Wes, and now I'm getting the lecture of a lifetime.

I should've called my mother instead and dealt with being grounded.

"I told you not to go to that party. Not to take her." Wes growls, slamming his hand on the steering wheel.

"Well, it's a good thing you're not our father."

"You know, Dex, you can be such a fucking asshole. I'm leaving for Washington in a month. I won't be able to pick you up all the fucking time. I won't be able to be with you guys to make sure you stay out of trouble. I'm not going to be able to make sure she's safe and that you're safe..."

"I can take care of Meadow!" I cut him off, pissed. I hate that he doesn't think I can take care of her. I'd been doing it long before him. Meadow always came to me first when she has a problem or a shoulder to cry on before they started dating. He knows better than anyone I would do anything for her, and I resent he would ever think otherwise.

"Like you did tonight?"

"We're fine, aren't we?" I spit back.

"Only because I was able to pick you up. What if I couldn't? What would you have done—walked? She's wasted and under your watch. When you told me that you fucking wouldn't go." He slams his hand on the steering wheel again, and even in the darkness of the car I can tell his face is blood red from his fury.

"Sorry that I wanted to hang out with my best friend for once without her damn boyfriend slobbering all over her," I yell back, and Meadow whimpers making us both stop. She doesn't wake and nuzzles her face back on my shoulder. The both of us sigh in relief knowing we didn't rouse her, and it seems to give Wes a chance to cool.

"You could've hung out at your house. Instead, you had to go out to some house party thirty miles out," Wes whispers.

"Oh my god. When did you turn into Mr. Stick up your ass? It was only months ago you would have been right with us at this party living it up. I get it, Mr. College boy. You got a job, you're doing better things. Next thing you'll do is marry Meadow and leave me behind."

"Is that what you think?" He turns to me, wide-eyed, and his jaw slack.

I don't answer him and look out the window. It's true. They have each other. Soon enough they won't need me. Meadow won't need me. She's already talking about following Wes to Washington. Then what? I'm left without my best friends.

"For what it's worth I am glad you called me, Dex. I want what's best for her. For you. If I can't be there, I guess I don't know."

"Don't get all fucking sappy on me now..." I turn back to him and laugh.

"Shut up—"

BAM!

The shriek of metal crushes and my body slams into the passenger side. My head hits the window with a loud whack making my ears ring. Glass shards fly pass my face and the car is spun around. It all happens so fast. I feel a heaviness on me, and I think it might be my friends on top of me. There's a loud horn making the throb of my head hurt more and making it even harder to think straight.

I need to check on Wes and Meadow.

I force myself to open my eyes…my vision is blurry, and I notice it is Meadow still pressed into my side. Her head is now along my chest, her one arm curled out along my leg and her other twisted back in the worst way, like a pretzel and it makes me cringe. She's bleeding—a lot, but I'm not sure where from. I say her name, but I'm not getting an answer. I touch her neck, checking for a pulse and I thank god when I feel a faint one.

Past her, at the driver side is a twisted mess of metal and tears leak from my eyes when I see Wes. His eyes are open, and he's bleeding from his mouth. "Wes? Wesley?" I gasp out. "Hang on, buddy. Help should be here soon."

"Dex, take care of her," Wes rasps out. His hand reaches out for Meadow but falls right back down.

"Don't talk like that, buddy…You'll be fine." I try to reassure him. I try to reassure myself. Though even in my haze, I'm not sure and my cheeks wet more, seeing my two favorite people so tangled up and hurting and I'm useless. "Wes, hang on. I think I hear sirens."

"Promise …me. "

"I promise but hang on. Promise me that."

I did my best to keep him talking, but after I made my

promise his eyes closed, and he fell silent. No matter how much I yelled at him, he wouldn't answer. Meadow wouldn't wake either. Soon the cops and the ambulance came to rescue us...well, they rescued everyone but Wes.

If I hadn't made him come pick us up that night. If I had only listened to him and not gone to that party, he would still be alive. I was being selfish as fuck because I missed hanging out with Meadow without them making out. It's my fault he was on the road when that drunk driver, who was going eighty, hit us. Wes didn't make it to the hospital. Meadow had a broken arm and a concussion that kept her under for two days. She still has no idea that Wes and I were fighting, or that he had asked me not to take her to the party. The memory fades when I see her GMC Terrain fly into the parking spot in front of the Garden City Restaurant.

I find a spot and slam the door on my Dodge, running after her before she can enter the restaurant. I grab her arm and spin her around. "What the hell is wrong with you?"

Fire flares out of her eyes to match the venom of my words. "Nothing! But something is about to be wrong with you and your balls if you don't unhand me." She wiggles herself out of my hold, but I grip her tighter, making her smack me in the chest. "Get off me."

"No, because you were speeding down the I-5. Were you trying to get yourself killed?"

"No, because believe it or not, I know how to fucking drive, asswipe. Your dad taught me. Remember? Just like he taught your dumb ass. Stop always treating me like I'm made of glass. I don't even get why you care. It's not like you give a fuck about me anyway."

I release her like she's on fire and she stumbles back.

"Now if you don't know why...then maybe it's you that needs to get their head out of their ass."

Her mouth drops open, but before she can say anything back, I move around her and storm inside the restaurant. I'm steaming. Does she really think I don't care about her? After everything? Talk about a fucking kick to the damn fucking teeth.

"Greene-Lexington Party," I tell the hostess and she leads me to the table where my parents and Meadow's mom await. My mom stands, engulfing me in a hug, followed by Meadow's mom, Valerie. "Where's my daughter? I thought for sure she'd be right behind you?" She peers over my shoulder and I look behind me, surprised the firecracker didn't come blowing in right behind me.

"She had to use the bathroom." My finger brushes my nose as I make up an excuse that would seem the most accurate.

Valerie squints at me, the same way Meadow does when she knows I'm hiding something. "Well, sit. We can order and start talking when she gets here."

I pull out my seat next to my father who pats my shoulder in a hello and asks me how work is going. I'm going on about this new building I'm designing downtown when the chair beside me scrapes across the floor. Meadow sits down, resting her elbow on the table, and puts her head in her hand, clearly avoiding looking at me. Her mother whispers something to her and she nods, and I make out the reply that she's fine.

From the corner of my eye, I see my mom throwing me a questioning look and my father leans back over to me. "Is everything okay with you two?" he probes, and I turn to him, picking up the menu, burying my head in it. This is going to be a long fucking meal.

"Everything is fine."

It wasn't fine, and it only got worse when we started going over the seating arrangements. When I found out Julian would be seated between Meadow and me, that string I was holding onto days ago, finally snapped.

Hell, who am I kidding, it snapped a while ago.

If she loved me like she said she did, she would be going with me and not Julian. Plus, this was Wes' parents anniversary dinner; she should be going with me or alone out of respect for Wes. Period.

So, fuck this. It might be stupid, and I might regret it later but there's no way I'm going to be some third fucking wheel. What does she expect?

"I forgot to mention I have a date for the event and need an extra chair at our table."

Chapter Nine

Meadow

As I watch Dexter storm inside the restaurant, I feel like the world around me has imploded. This last week has been one of the hardest I can remember since Pickle's death. Every day has been like going through the normal motions in what feels like an alternate universe. The moment I saw Dexter and Kayleigh at my office with her arms around him, everything I knew felt lost. The person I trusted most in the world had betrayed me.

Even if in some fucked up way this was his plan to make me jealous or trying to one-up me, he'd had his chance to apologize by now. Or at least explain why he did that shit. He knew what Kayleigh was to me—how she made me feel—and yet because I was *'dating'* Julian it seemed to be okay for him to 'date' her or whatever he was doing.

I mean after one lunch he was defending her to me. What the fuck?

Maybe it all didn't matter anyway. I told him I loved

him. This time I know he remembers it. *I* remember it, even if he doesn't think I do. When he told he couldn't love me and I didn't deserve him, I knew at that point, no matter what I tried to do I was never going to change his mind. Dexter Greene is one of the most stubborn men on this planet and once he's made up his mind, that's it. Not even this odd rage of jealousy was going to change it.

If Dexter Greene truly wanted me, he had his chance to make his move—instead maybe I thrust him into the arms of another woman—a woman I hated.

Hell, I don't even know what he's doing right now. I haven't been able to look him in the eye all week. The morning after I drunk confessed—again—that I loved Dexter, I called Julian and ended the 'plan.' I couldn't keep it up knowing he knew how I truly felt. It was out there. The ball is in his court. If he needed time to deal with whatever he was going through with Wes, I was willing to wait.

I only wish he could've seen that I wasn't ever with him. That Julian never came to the house nor did I ever stay at his place. The only time Dexter even saw us kiss was because he had been spying that first night when we were out on the porch. That when we went Karaoke, we didn't even hang out. Like it was the *lamest* and *tames*t dating ever.

Damn it, Dex. Why are you closing us out?

"Are you okay, hun?" A gentle hand touches my shoulder, and I peer down at a white-haired lady now standing beside me.

"Huh? Um yeah?"

"You don't look so good. Here." She shuffles through her purse and pulls out a tissue from a little

Kleenex bag and hands it to me. That's when I realized my cheeks are wet from crying. Shit, now I feel like an idiot.

How long have I been standing here?

"Thank you." I take the tissue from her and wipe my face.

"You're welcome, sweetie. Why don't you take the whole thing." She shoves the little plastic bag in my hand, and I giggle at her. "Now if this is about a boy, and you need me to give *him* a reason to cry, you let me know." She winks, and holds up her walking cane, making me laugh.

"I might take you up on that." I deserved what Dexter said to me moments ago, but I would pay good money to see this lady go after him for the hell of it.

"Mom, what are you doing?" An older gentleman with salt and pepper hair comes out of the restaurant and spies me curiously.

"Just making a new friend." She winks at me again and moves towards her son. "Are we all set?"

"Yeah?" he says unsure, still eyeing me. I wipe my eyes, having no clue if I look like a hot mess still. "You okay?"

"She's fine, Gerald. She needed a good laugh. Right, hun?"

"Yes, thank you again for the tissues. I should get inside anyways to meet my family."

"You take care, dear. Chin up." She pats me on the shoulder before her son takes her elbow leading her away from me.

When I enter the restaurant, I head to the bathroom to clean my face off before any of my family can see me.

I try to take the old lady's advice of 'chin up,' but I'd much rather have her cane, which does make me chuckle. I splash a little more water on my face and dry it off.

I make my way to the table and see Dex making small talk to his dad. His mother, Joy, spots me and waves me over. Sadly, there's only one empty seat available and that's between Dex and my mother. I brush my hair to the left, so Dex can't see my face as I sit down, and then scoot my seat in closer to my mom.

Not that I think Dex would care right now, but I don't want him to know that I've been crying. He will be able to tell, even though I did my best to clean my face. I deserved his harshness when it came to my speeding. If anyone gets on me about it, it's Dex. Five miles over the limit and the man has a coronary.

"Sorry, it took me so long," I tell my mother and she takes my hand.

"Is everything okay?"

"Everything is fine."

Beside me, Dex mumbles the same words to his father matching my enthusiasm.

Mom narrows her eyes and leans in closer to me. "Sweetie, you know you can tell me anything. I can tell you've been crying." She brushes my cheek and my eyes close tightly.

Well, so much for trying to hide anything.

"Maybe later," I whisper back. "But I'm okay for now. Really. Can we order now?"

She nods and I'm grateful that she drops it. We order our meals and go over the final arrangements for the anniversary party. At first, this was to be a surprise for Martha and Frank, but my mother and Joy aren't ones to keep secrets, so the couple knew about the party within a week after the idea was hatched. However, the five of us are still planning everything as if it were one.

"Okay, so I made up the seating chart last night. Look it over and tell me what you think. I figured ten tables of six, then the main table will have ten." My mother hands me the seating chart and as I look it over, Julian's name glares at me. *Shit.* He's now sitting next to me at the main table. What the fuck is this change? Dexter rips the paper from me and I lean over to my mother needing to know how she even knew I was going out with him. I haven't told her anything that was going on.

"Wait, why is Julian between me and Dexter?" I whisper to my mother and she twists her eyebrows at me.

"Aren't you guys dating?" I feel as if my eyes are bulging out of my sockets. I never wanted that to get back to our mothers because I knew it would be blown out of proportion.

"Who told you that?"

"Joy. She said Dexter told her. Are you not?"

My eyes close from the sudden throbbing inside my head. If I didn't already have enough stress and weight on my shoulders now, I feel like one of Dexter's buildings has been dropped on them. "No. We're not, never were."

"Oh." My mom frowns.

Beside me Dexter clears his throat, grabbing mine and my mother's attention. "I forgot to mention I have a *date* for the event and need an extra chair at our table." He glares at me and my heart sinks into my stomach.

"You do? Why didn't you tell me?" Joy asks her son, clearly shocked by the news. Her eyes flit over in my direction.

"It's new. And who wants to be alone at one of these things, right?"

"Well, what's her name?"

I know what's coming. He's bringing *her* so he can stick it to me when he's the one who unexpectedly caused this whole mess. But it doesn't mean I'm prepared the second her name leaves his lips. "Kayleigh."

I toss my napkin on the table and turn to my friend who has twisted the knife in my heart deeper. "Dex, can I talk to you?"

He smirks at me and I'm so close to wanting to lay him out on this damn table. It brings back a fond memory of a time when I was eight and wrestled him in a Chuck E. Cheese for stealing all my tickets, but I digress. "Sure. Excuse us."

We both rise from the table and I take the lead going outside. Once we make it past the double doors into the fresh air, I find myself walking to the end of the parking lot, away from any possible spectators.

I fold my arms across my chest, bracing myself for a fight.

Okay, I'm doing it in an attempt to not knock him out.

"You can't bring Kayleigh to this party."

"Why not? You're bringing Julian." He spits out the words and I roll my eyes. I'm so sick of this.

"Julian was already on the list along with all our friends before he was seated next to me, Dex."

"He didn't know Wes," he argues and I want to scream—Scratch that. I want to strangle him and hopefully free the stupid man child out of him.

"He knows Frank and Martha and us. Stop this. I'm not the one who told your mom about me going out with

Julian, you did that. Otherwise, he would still be at the table across from us. Stop acting like a damn child. It can be fixed. Instead, you invite Kayleigh, for what, to hurt me? Again?"

He shrugs. "Well, it's done now anyway."

I gape at him. He's unbelievable. This isn't my Dexter. My best friend wouldn't go out of his way to hurt me, to spite me, no matter how he was feeling.

This isn't us. Period.

"Where is my friend?"

"Where's mine?" he hisses back. "You're the one who thinks I don't give a shit about you right? Well, I guess I'm only proving that to you."

My head drops to look at my feet, filled with my own guilt. "I'm sorry for saying that, but you still have no right to keep acting like this."

"Like what?"

"A jealous Neanderthal," I mumble.

"Excuse me?"

My head snaps up and his eyes squint at me like I lost my mind. If I didn't feel so lost and broken hearted I would laugh. I only have myself to blame for most of this and now I'm coming to realize, I can't do it anymore. I thought it would be easy because I thought he loved me and needed a push. But my heart has taken such a beating that if this keeps going on, it'll be nothing more than dust by the time this is all said and done.

"You're acting like a jealous Neanderthal and I can't do this anymore," I clarify and find myself folding, giving up on trying to win Dexter Greene's heart. Completely. Accepting that I'll only be his best friend and nothing more.

Well, that's if we make it through this.

"Can't do what?" he whispers and for the first time since we got here, I see a crack in his bad boy act.

"I love you. Like I'm really truly madly *in l*ove with you." His eyes grow wide and they dart around the empty parking lot. I don't know why he's taking my words as such a shock. He already knew this, but maybe he never expected me to say this out loud, especially here and now. "I'm in love with you, Dex," I repeat to make myself extra clear because he appears to be oblivious to the words.

"Meadow…I um..." I hold out my hand to stop him.

"Before you give me your excuses to why you *can't 'be in love with me,'*" I snap, making him shift nervously on his feet, something he used to do when he was caught doing something wrong, "I have something I need to tell you."

He nods and I take a steady breath about to lay all my cards on the table. Everything I'm about to admit will change our friendship forever. But at this point, our friendship has already taken the hit with all the secrets we've been keeping.

"I made up this whole plan about going out with Julian because I thought when you saw me with him you would realize that you are *in love* with me. That you loved me more than your best friend. Everyone around us could see it but *you*. I felt the change between us building for a long time and I had hoped that maybe you did too. I thought it would be easy. Instead, you turned into a jealous Neanderthal. And that was all fine and dandy for a while. Sometimes it was cute. But god damn you were so fucking blind not to see what was in front of you. That you couldn't see that me and Julian never went out more than three times. We never kissed, except that one time when he knew you were looking."

"I don't believe this..." He turns away from me, covering his mouth.

"I didn't know what else to do. I felt lost. I only did it because you told me you loved me on my birthday and then basically the next second you told me you couldn't." That grabs his attention and he turns back to me, gaping, but he doesn't say anything. "Before I brought Julian in, I flirted with you more. I came into your bed with sexy PJ's and you treated me like I had a disease. You mentioned the thought of us as a married couple, disgusting. There wasn't much I could do, outside of telling you I loved you again, that you wouldn't find abnormal for us. So Mel thought if I started dating again you would see what you were missing because we both had stopped. Instead, you turned into a jackass, treated your friend like shit because he wasn't you. Well, that's how I summed that all up. Then we had that moment in the kitchen...which yes, was ruined by Julian calling, but hey there was still a moment."

He scratches his nose and looks away from me again.

"Are you going to deny it?" I holler, wanting to shake him so I can get anything out of him before I crumble to the ground in defeat.

"I don't know, Meadow. You still took his call."

"Because you told me to take the call and then you walked away acting like a jealous asshole," I scream and poke him in the chest.

"You then went on a date with him the next day. What did you want from me, Meadow? You made your choice." His voice cracks and I can make out the hurt swimming in his eyes.

"Maybe it was a mistake on my end. Maybe I shouldn't have ever brought Julian into the equation. I'm to blame for that. But maybe if you sat down and actually asked about Julian or used your head maybe we could have talked, but you kind of forgot about him being your friend too and I found that kind of disgusting."

"He wasn't good for you and he was fake anyway, so I did know better." He smirks. *And there's* the cocky asshole coming out to play again.

"So, if I can't have Wes or *you*...then who am I supposed to date?"

"I don't know. I figure I'll know when I meet them."

"You're such an ass. So I'm supposed to be single till you pick my prince charming? Thing is I want you...or I did…hell, I'm not sure anymore. Because all you seem to do is rip my heart open again and again." My chin quivers and my voice breaks from the unshed tears that I'm doing everything in my power to contain.

"That's not what I'm trying to do." He steps towards me, reaching out for me and I instantly step back. I *can't* have him touching me right now.

"Isn't it though? I told you I loved you after karaoke. I know I was drunk, but so were you. I figured maybe you would be honest again like you were on my birthday. And again, you admitted to me you couldn't *love* me." My voice raises and his eyes bulge as I declare the biggest secret of all. "I know it has something to do with Wes. Maybe in your mind you still have to work something out with his death. What, I don't know. So, I decided to let it go. I called the whole thing off with Julian and I thought maybe, somehow, we could work through these Wes issues you have or whatever is going on. Our friendship is more important. I mean I had been dealing with these feelings for a year, what was a little bit longer, right? But you had lunch with Kayleigh. Then you defended *her* to me. I couldn't even look at you. Then today. I don't know Dex, maybe I don't know you after all."

"Wait, wait back up. Your *birthday*?"

I chuckle dryly. "You know not everyone gets blackout drunk and forgets like you do. There was a reason why I was so mad at you and throwing shit around for days, Dex. Do you not realize how much it killed me when I realized you forgot we had sex?"

His mouth opens and closes like a fish, and he stumbles backwards a bit in his state of shock. "What do you mean we had sex? We had *sex*?" His voice croaks and his hands fly to his hair. "Oh my god, Meadow. I'm sorry."

"Why?" I snap, feeling the blood in my veins boil and about to blow. "We had a pretty good time. I mean you did at the time. You told me that you were in love with me. In love with me! We both proclaimed our love for each other! This is so much deeper than you think! Then the next thing I know, you're telling me, 'you can't,' 'you can't,' before you passed out. The next morning, you clearly had no memory of it because you acted normal, like nothing ever happened between us! Maybe I should have stayed in bed with you so you could remember our night together. I was so scared that you would reject me if I had spilled it out to you. So as I said, I thought it would be fun to help you see that you did love me, which is why I flirted, and the main reason I brought in Julian. I was hoping it would click the memory banks and you would become like a possessive man and claim me as yours, but it didn't work. It's my fault. But I ended up being right because if I had told you, you would have rejected me."

"I'm sorry, Meadow."

"Stop saying that!" I screech.

"The last thing I ever wanted to do was hurt you. You know our friendship means everything to me. What can I do to fix this? I won't bring Kayleigh. That was stupid and I'm sorry."

"This isn't about Kayleigh anymore, Dex."

"Then what. What can I do?"

I swallow the hard lump now piled in my throat. It's now or never and it might be a little unfair, but it needs to be done and I need to know for myself.

"I think this is your chance now. I know how you feel. How you truly feel. I know what's holding you back and I can understand it in a way. But this is it, Dex, now or never. Do you or do you not *love* me?"

He closes his eyes and is silent for a moment. I know he wants to say something, but what comes out of his mouth pisses me off more... "I don't deserve you," he mumbles.

"That's not what I asked you!" I snap. "I asked if you loved me."

"Meadow...I...can't... it wouldn't be right."

"For who?"

"For Wes. For You."

"Wes isn't here! And me? I'm in love with you, damn it! There's something between us, Dex. Something more! Why do you keep on fighting it?" I seethe and wonder how Wes can be held over our heads at this point! He's gone. Though he'll always be a part of us, I don't know how we'll ever heal if he's like a ghost looming over us, never letting us go, never letting us move on.

"Doesn't matter and if you can't get that, that's where the problem is."

I look up to the sky trying to keep my tears from falling. I'm emotionally and physically drained. I can't do this anymore. My whole body is trembling, and I feel as though I'm about to be sick. Around us, I feel the walls of our friendship start to crumble. They're no longer the strongest of concrete that had always held us together. They aren't going to be enough to make it through this storm we're going through right now.

"You're right. I don't get it. At least from your point of view. I thought I did, but obviously, there's something I'm missing and you won't tell me. Thing is, I don't think I care anymore." I suck in all the pain, all the hurt, and then blow it out. There's nothing left inside my heart, it's hollow. Dexter Greene emptied what was left of me. "Fine. I accept now that you can't love me. It is what it is. At least now I know for sure."

Dex rubs his wrinkled forehead, "Listen, Meadow, I'm sorr—"

"Stop!" I hold my hand up. "Just stop. I'm going back inside to tell everyone I have a headache. Then I'll go home. Don't worry. I'll have them move Julian and maybe myself." I spin on my heel needing to get away from him, away from the devastation he caused my heart.

This is why they always say you never cross the line from friends to lovers because it's almost impossible to turn back. How do I forget Dex took my heart and disintegrated it into ashes?

I enter the restaurant, not even caring that my face is a mess and that I'm crying. Our parents are going to ask a hundred questions and I have no answers to give them. All I know is I have to get out of here. I need to be alone with my broken heart. When I get to the table, Joy and my mother quickly stand and without a word, my mom gathers me in her arms. "What happened?"

"Not here. I need to go." I wipe my face to rid the residue of my tear stains. "And can you please move Julian back to where he was with our friends. We're not dating. There was some miscommunication."

"I knew it," Joy says coming in and rubbing my back. "I know that couldn't have been...Is that what has you so upset, sweetie?"

I don't say anything, but there's no denying anything to the two women that I consider my mothers. One biological and the other God-sent. Not that they couldn't smell something wrong between me and Dexter the second we walked in the door.

Plus, look at me. I'm a hot mess.

"I can talk to him, hun. That boy has been jealous of the mention of you and Julian since he found out. Also, I was hoping this would push him...I didn't expect him to get a date. He's always been stubborn!"

"Joy!" my mother admonishes.

"What? He's in denial."

"What are you girls going on about?" Thomas says leaning back in his chair, sipping his water. "Why don't you all sit down? You're drawing attention"

"No, I have to go."

"Honey, what is going on with you two?"

"Nothing that we can't work out. We always do. It'll

be fine, I'll be fine." I try to convince them, but it's my heart and myself that I'm trying to convince. "But can you guys email me everything else that needs to be handled by next weekend?"

"Of course, sweetie. Do you want me to come with you?" my mom says gently.

"No, I need to be alone right now."

"Okay." My mom smooths my hair back and when I look up, I see Dexter walking in. He looks as bad as I feel, with his hair standing on all ends and the top of his blazer unbuttoned.

"Don't be too rough on him. All of this is not his fault." I give both women a small smile and pick up my purse. "I'll talk to you guys later."

I step away from the table and as I breeze past Dexter his fingers brush my arm. I'm mildly disappointed when he doesn't say anything, but what did I expect—he can't.

He can't.

Chapter Ten

Dexter

When Meadow walks past me, I don't think I've ever seen such a look of pure crumbling devastation on her face—at least, not since Wes died. The vacant eyes, the tear-stained cheeks, her quaking shoulders, I did that. I hurt her. Ripped her heart out, like I did that night seven years ago when Wes died, all because of me.

But I did the right thing.

She has to know a relationship between her and me isn't something that can ever happen.

Then why does it make me feel like shit? To know I lost the best thing and the most important person in my life.

"Dexter William Greene! What did you do to her?" my mother hisses quietly, with her hands on her hips. She's trying not to grab the whole attention of the restaurant, but she still manages to make a few heads turn from the tables around us.

"Mom, I…" I have no idea what to say or how much information Meadow gave them.

"Joy, leave the boy alone." My father interrupts and I thank god for his peace saving efforts.

"I want to help." My mom sits back in her chair and Valerie nods agreeing to the assessment. If I don't get out of here soon, they'll both have me under the bright lights of an interrogation room till I confess.

"No, you want to dig for information because Meadow didn't give you all of it." He chuckles. "But right now it's obvious he needs to go after her."

"Actually, I don't know about that." I disagree. If I don't tell her what she wants to hear right now, Meadow Lexington might chop me up into little pieces.

I slept with her and I don't remember. Right there is enough for her to have my balls. Much less that I didn't tell her I loved her back.

"Well, either way, you're no good to us. And I'm saving you from your mother and Valerie. Now go."

"Thanks, Dad."

With a quick goodbye, I hightail it out of the restaurant. When I get to my truck, my head falls back on the headrest as I replay the events of today. It's as if a tornado came roaring through and exposed every secret and pent up emotion we've been hiding. Now there's this huge mess left to clean up.

The place I need to start at and uncover some more truths is with Julian. I pull out my phone and find his contact, stabbing each letter into the keyboard as I text him.

Where you at?
We need to talk A.S.A.P

I'm thankful that his reply is instant.

> *Julian: I'm at the office.*
> *What's up?*

I'll be there in ten.

> *Julian: Dude,*
> *what's going on?*

It's about Meadow.

> *Julian: I see. Alright.*
> *See you in ten.*

Pulling out of the lot, I head down the highway to my office building on South Street. The whole trip, I try to process what the hell I'm going to say to him, but the only thing I can think about is the soul-crushing look on Meadow's face. I barge into SJD designs and race down the halls lined with glass walls of our offices. When I reach Julian's, he's busy drafting at his desk.

I clear my throat, and cross my arms over my chest, widening my stance in front of him.

Julian throws down his pencil and rocks back in his chair when he sees me. "Do I need to have security ready for this visit? Or do you come in peace?"

"I want to know why. Why would you fuck with me like you did?"

"I see she finally told you everything."

"She did. Now tell me!" I bellow, and I hand it to the motherfucker when he doesn't flinch.

"Because it's as clear as day you both are in love with

each other and you needed help to fucking see it." He shrugs, not giving a fuck that he went behind my back.

"You should've told me." I pound my fist to my chest.

"Give me a break, man. It was clear as day to everyone else how you both felt about each other. Because trust me, you wouldn't be here sulking and upset if you didn't feel the way that you do." He smirks like he's not affected by any of this. Like he's proud of what he did.

"You shouldn't have stuck your business in it."

"Maybe not, but she came to me. The girl is hopelessly in love with you and felt stuck. She told me what happened on her birthday."

"She told you!" I hiss, shaking my head. "I don't believe this." Did she go around telling everyone about my drunk ass sleeping with her and then forgetting? Way to boost up my self-esteem and make me feel even more like an ass.

Thanks, Meadow.

"Listen, she didn't do it to be spiteful. Believe it or not, I was being her friend and Meadow had her own damn worries about everything. About you rejecting her because of something to do with Wes? She said that you said that you *can't* love her?"

I pinch the bridge of my nose and close my eyes. Hearing those words out loud from someone else is bizarre. Though it doesn't make them any less true.

I can't love her, not in the way she wants me to. Not in the way that I want to.

"She thought you needed to see it. I swore in the office after our "first date" when your head was about to explode you would have taken her from me then, but you didn't. So what the fuck is going on? You should be wherever she is, not here with me."

"I'm trying to make sense of everything. But also because she's right, I can't be with her."

"What?" He scoffs, pushing back from his chair and stands. "That's fucking bullshit! Why the fuck not?"

"It's not bullshit. It's the fucking truth. You wouldn't understand."

"Try me." He rounds his desk and inches closer to me.

"I don't have to explain anything to you. I only came here wanting to know how someone that was my friend could do what you did."

"Because you need someone to fucking help you." He jabs his finger in my chest and I knock it away. But it doesn't shut him up. "You love that girl and for some damn reason you're being stupid and not allowing it."

"Because you don't get it. You *don't* fucking get it!" I shout and in an instant, Julian's nameplate goes flying across the room and clatters to the floor.

"Then make me get it, dude!" Julian grabs my shoulders and shakes me like a disobedient child. "All I've been fucking doing this whole time is being yours and Meadow's friend. That's fucking all. Let me do that. Tell me what the fuck is going on. Because obviously, this is bigger than actually *not* loving her."

I pry his hands off me and shove him back. My fingers push through my hair as I collapse into the chair in front of his desk. The fight in me leaves and I suddenly feel drained. "You're right…" I mumble.

"Just tell me, Dex. What the fuck is going on with you?"

With a heavy sigh, I realize I came here to start cleaning up a mess. Secrets are what put Meadow and me in this disaster in the first place and I'm holding onto the biggest one of all.

"You know what I think about most of the time when I look at Meadow…" I pause, my elbows falling to my knees and I tug on my hair till it hurts, wishing I could pull out all the strands. "Every time I look at her, I remember that she should be happy with Wes, with like a hundred babies. Because thanks to me I killed the ending she was supposed to have with him."

"What?" Julian plops in the seat in front of me, frowning. "What are you talking about? How is Wes' death your fault? You guys were hit by a drunk driver."

"We were, but if I hadn't been such a dick to him and brought Meadow to that party in the Valley to spite him when he asked me not to, we wouldn't have been on that road in the first place. I missed hanging out with my best friend alone, so Meadow and I got trashed. Then when it ended, we were left with no ride. There were no cabs or anyone available to take us back. My only option to get home besides calling our parents was Wes….and I kind of wanted to say 'fuck you' to him." My eyes close and my lips tuck in from the sharp knife piercing in my gut knowing that was the main reason for it all.

I wanted to show him that I could still do whatever I wanted with Meadow even though they were dating, that she was my friend and I could take care of her too. We could have fun and she would be okay under my watch while he was in college. Though, under my watch nearly got her killed and ultimately did kill Wes.

"So you see, we wouldn't have been there if he didn't

come and pick us up because I was being an asshole. I don't deserve her because I fucked up everything she could've had. She could've had everything. The perfect fucking life."

"Dex...you can't possibly—"

"It doesn't even matter," I snap, cutting him off. "Loving her is betraying Wes. I also took his life away from him, you know. He loved her so damn much. It was freakin' sickening some days. Now I feel like a bigger tool knowing I slept with her. More so that I don't even remember it. I used her. Wes would definitely kick my ass because I would kick my own. I hated any guy that couldn't compare to Wes. I made him that promise before he died that I would take care of her and that was to keep her away from low lives that would only use her."

"Like me?" Julian chuckles, and my head bounces up to look at him.

"Yeah. No offense."

"Oh. Now you claim no offense?" He rolls his eyes and puts his hand on my shoulder. "Dude you wanted to kick my ass every time you walked in this office. And it had nothing to do with your promise to Wes. It's because you're in love with her and you don't want anyone else to have her. Admit it."

"I don't deserve her. Why can't you get that?"

"I do. And I think it's all twisted and confusing too. Does she know any of this?"

"She knows about the accident, of course, but she has no clue that Wes and I were fighting about the party and that he didn't want us to go. Nobody does."

Julian's eyes go wide, and he falls back in his chair. "Nobody. Not even his parents? Or yours?"

"No."

"Holy shit, dude. You know nobody would blame you, right?"

"That's a crock of shit. If I told Martha and Frank the truth, they would kill me. I mean they knew he was working that night—and he wasn't there the whole time—I don't know." I run my hands through my hair. I never talked to them about it. They assumed he came for us and I left it at that. How was I supposed to tell them I ultimately put their son in harm's way and got him killed? "I wish I could go back in time and never have gone to that stupid party. Or maybe called him sooner to get us or even just taken a few minutes longer to get in the car. Hell, sometimes I think it should've been me that night because it was my fault…"

"Fuck man! You can't mean that." Julian leans in concerned.

"You didn't know Meadow and Wes. And Wes wouldn't have treated her like I did today."

"Maybe not. But Wes isn't holding onto seven years of fucking blame on his damn shoulders. I still don't get why you think you are responsible anyway?"

"Didn't you hear a fucking word I fucking said?" I rise to my feet seething and Julian is on his just as quick.

"I did! I heard it all. I do get what you're saying, but also—like damn it, Dex. You should've unloaded this shit years ago. You were sixteen. And what I'm about to say to you... I'm sorry, but I'm going to be frank with you, and I'm not going to baby you through your grief. I'm not Meadow. Maybe if you told her what the fuck happened she'd be wrapping you in her damn arms, but guess what, bro? I'm not sugar coating it. Now sit the fuck down and chill. Because do you want your friend back? At least that much?"

I nod. "Yeah. Of course, I do."

"Then listen because you're going to need to get over this bullshit blame you have. Then you're going to admit that you love Meadow and tell her your damn sorry. Then figure out how to win her back if you have to."

I plop back in the chair and my head falls in my hands, knowing maybe this is what I needed. Someone that isn't so close to the bullshit. Amazingly, it already feels like a fifty-pound weight has lifted off my chest telling someone else what happened that night.

"I get why you feel responsible. Maybe you shouldn't have gone to that party, but you did. You were sixteen. But you still did the responsible thing and called someone sober to drive you. You could have gotten into a car with anyone. You could have driven. You could have walked and got hit. In the end, a drunk driver hit you guys! It all fucking sucks, Dexter. You didn't fucking ask for that asshole to do it! You didn't wish for it to happen! It was an accident! You and Meadow could have died too. But none of this was your fault."

"But I could've just stayed at my house with Meadow."

"I get it. I do, but Dexter you can't punish yourself for it. It's not a way to live and you need to forgive yourself for it. I think you need to fucking talk to someone. Obviously, this guilt is killing you, man. And it's going to stop you from the one thing *you want,* and *you deserve*…And you need to start by telling her."

But do I truly deserve her?

"I think she would hate me forever if she knew what

really happened."

"Really? Are we talking about the same girl? Meadow Lexington? Please. Just tell her what you told me. I'm about a thousand times sure she would understand. I don't know how she wouldn't." I open my mouth and he puts up his hand automatically stopping me. "And if you say anything on the lines of saying you killed her boyfriend, I will knock you on your ass, Greene. You've had this on your shoulders for so long, *you* didn't know any better."

"You don't have to because you said it for me." I smirk. "But I will. Whenever I can get her to talk to me again. It's already been one hell of a week."

"Oh yes. I heard all about the Kayleigh thing. What the fuck were you thinking?" He laughs, shaking his head.

"No fucking clue. I was being a dick. I don't know." I groan and wonder if out of all the things if I'll be forgiven for *that* mistake. Maybe Meadow was right, and I was acting like a jealous Neanderthal because I did want her to feel everything I was going through with her dating Julian. "So, what now?"

"What is it that you want? Something close to the friendship you had or something more?"

I'm silent for a moment, thinking back to the past few weeks. Hell, the last year. How everyone agrees that we are so in love with each other—to the fact that maybe I'm indeed blind in my feelings for her. It would be stupid for me to doubt that I wouldn't want *something* with Meadow. She's been my entire life since I can remember. Every memory revolves around her and life would cease to exist without her.

It's just I'm not sure how to admit it all out loud.

There's still this creep of betrayal in the form of Wes' face. It's this hard line between wrong and right. I just know I have to do something if I want Meadow to stay in my life because I fear I might have pushed her away too hard this time.

I can already feel the fortress she's put up around us.

"First, I've got to get her to talk to me. See if she is willing to give me a chance to make things up to her."

"Well, she came up with a plan to help you try to get your hard head out of your ass. It worked to an extent. Maybe you need to do something similar."

"What do you have in mind?"

"It's not the greatest of ideas. I've never had to woo a girl before."

"You're an ass," I want to smack the smug look off his face, "and this is why I knew you and Meadow…"

"Fuck off." He plants a punch to my arm making me grit my teeth from the dead arm he just gave me. *Fucker.* "Do you want my help or not?"

"Fine, but I think I'm pretty good at wooing already."

"Alright. Only make sure it doesn't involve another woman, especially Kayleigh."

I punch him back in the right arm, hoping to return the same pain he inflicted on me and head out of the office.

When I get back home, Meadow's car isn't in its normal parking spot. I figured she wouldn't be here, but I had held out hope that maybe she would be so we could try to talk. I pull out my phone and send her a text asking her where she is. Though as I expect, she doesn't answer me in her usual timely manner.

I'm not sure what makes me go straight to her bedroom, but I have this uncomfortable feeling telling me something is up. As I flick on the light, my suspicions are right when I spot clothes thrown all over my usually neat freak of a best friend's bed and her dresser drawer is hanging open.

"Fuck," I yell to the empty room and yank on my hair. The tornado that ripped through our friendship, has officially wiped out the one thing we had safe: Our home. She's gone and I have no idea when she's coming back.

Or if she would even want to come back.

This had been a bigger disaster than I ever saw coming, and I wasn't sure if my plan was going to be enough to win her over.

I move to her dresser and close the drawers. On top, Meadow has a collection of pictures from throughout the years, including one from her birthday in a crazy pink and blue bedazzled frame. I'm not even sure at what point this picture was taken, but Meadow's legs are wrapped around my waist and she has one arm around my neck, while her other fist pumps the air. She looks so happy as she smiles into the camera and I appear—I move the frame closer to my face to take a good look at myself. I'm staring right at her, looking like a lovesick fool. Sure, I was probably shit faced at the time, but even right now I would be stupid to deny it:

That I'm *in* love with Meadow Lexington.

I take the picture to the bed and stare at for a while longer, trying to see if it could help trigger the black hole of the night. The longer I stare, the only thing I can recall now is how great her boobs looked and how perfect her ass was that night. Especially in this picture with the way I was holding her, because her dress has ridden up, exposing the bottom of that tight little ass.

Damn, why the fuck did I have to blackout?

But then where would we be now?

Setting the picture aside, I pull out my phone to text her. Needing to know she's okay. Needing to hear from her.

Please at least let me
know you're okay.
I'm sorry.

Five minutes pass, then ten, then thirty, and still nothing.

I'm back in my room, pacing the length. I've tried calling and it rang and then went to voicemail each time I did. So, I try texting again.

Come on Meadow.
Please. You left upset and
I'm worried. Just tell me
anything...that you're fine,
that you're alive...
anything...

I'll take her damn smart mouth even if right now it

would be something that would hurt me. Even if she told me she was with some guy. When I don't get an answer, I text Mel, knowing that's the person she's more than likely with.

Mel if you hear from Meadow
can you please let me know
if she's okay?

Instead of waiting for a reply, I text the next people on my list of usual suspects: Randy, Steph, and Steve. Twenty minutes later and none of them have heard from her today.

I fall back on my bed and rake my hands through my hair, feeling like a complete fuck up.

Chapter Eleven

Meadow

Mel flings open the door of her apartment and pulls me in along with my duffle bag. The door closes, my bag falls to the floor, she grips me into a tight hug, and I lose it all over again.

"Are you sure it's okay that I stay here for a bit?" I hiccup. Shit, I thought I was finally done crying. But now being squeezed to death by my best girlfriend brings it all back.

"Girl, you know you can always stay here anytime. But what happened?"

"I'll tell you, but do you think I could have some wine—or tequila. Or anything."

"I got you. Go sit down, boo." She wipes my cheek with her sleeved hand from her oversized sweater. I nod and move over to the couch where I curl into a tiny ball on the corner of her navy-blue, leather couch.

Her black lab, Angel, is right at my side, nudging her head into my hand wanting to be pet. Her way of giving comfort. Mel comes back over with a full glass of red wine and I prop myself up enough to take it from her. She sits beside me and rubs my back.

"Okay, I don't think I've seen you like this before, girl. What happened?"

I sip the sweet wine and sniff back my tears. Only to know they will start again when I tell her what happened. "I told Dex that I loved him. This time sober. And he told me once again that he can't."

"What? Why?"

I take another sip of the wine and then place it down on the side table. Angel moves her head lifting my arm, encouraging me that it's okay, as another tear slips from my eye. "He said it wouldn't be right because of Wes and if I couldn't understand why then that was the problem. I told him fine and, *well,* here I am now. I need to be away from him. Looking at him is hard enough. It's been difficult enough to deal with what he did with Kayleigh, but now.... "

"Yeah, that was a dick move," Mel mutters, rolling her eyes.

"You're telling me. That's what got us here today. When we were at lunch...*oh god.* We were going over the last minute seating arrangements for Frank and Martha's anniversary party. And I guess he had told his mom I was with Julian, so they had moved him next to me. The fucking jealous ape thought it would be brilliant to think he could invite Kayleigh to the party. I led him outside and I couldn't take it anymore. He's just been—*ahhh.* " My hands clench together in a strangle motion wishing it was his neck. "I spilled the truth about the plan, about Julian, and being in love with him...and he told me 'can't' for the third time."

The tears spill once again from my cheeks, like I

figured they would. I'm pissed at myself for still crying about this.

"Third?" Mel questions and I curl myself back into a ball as I tell her what happened after karaoke last weekend. She listens, with cringes and gasps, and it's no wonder she thinks my life is a soap opera. "Do you think you guys will work this out?"

"Of course we will. Eventually." I sigh. *We have to.* The last thing I ever want to do is lose him. It's just I need the stabbing pain in my heart to stop first. "We've been friends forever. I need time to get over him. To, I guess, realize we will never be more. I don't know how to do that right this second, but we'll figure it out I'm sure."

"Or maybe in that time he'll finally get it through his thick skull that he *can* love you."

"I don't know, and right now, I'm done worrying about it."

Mel slips her arm around me, "I'm sorry. You can stay as long as you need. And I'll be happy to kick his butt if you want because I don't get it."

Me either.

Once I'm tucked under the covers, I let the tears rain down my face. I punch my pillow, and for the first time in a long time, I curse that drunk driver for taking Wesley from me. My heart aches, knowing how much I miss him. *Especially right now.*

Wes would know what to do to help fix this. Even if we weren't together—he could fix everything. He was always good at that. He was kind of that extra glue that kept us all together. The problem solver. When Dex and I didn't know something, we went to him.

If Wes was here right now, I doubt I would be here crying and wondering what is wrong with me. Wondering why I can't be *loved.*

I also doubt that the person I love would be struggling so much because he thinks he needs to honor his cousin, his best friend's relationship, even in death. Hell, I don't even know what is truly going through the man's head and it's clear he'll never tell me.

Why couldn't this all be simple?

"I hate you for leaving us!" I yell to the empty bedroom, then find myself crying harder. Now, I hate myself for telling my first love, my best friend, such words.

"I don't hate you, Wes. I hate all this. If you didn't leave, I wouldn't be in love with Dex. Then that really sucks thinking I could never love him, but then again, I wouldn't be here, crying like a baby, now would I?" I wipe my nose and the tears keep falling down my cheeks.

I could have been married to Wes and had kids with him by now. But even if Dex can't love me, the only image I see for my happily ever after is being with Dexter Greene.

"I don't know what I'm supposed to do. Your cousin is driving me insane. Can you drop him a sign or something? Give me a damn sign of what I need to do?

Please? Or help give me some strength to make it through this? Anything." I beg Wes' ghost, the one that seems to be haunting us.

I pray for Dex because maybe he still needs peace. It had been the one thing I had thought I helped him with, like he did with me. But I guess I was wrong.

Maybe I don't deserve him because I let him down when he needed me the most.

"Meadow, I have a delivery for you." Ariel, the head receptionist, pokes her head into my office wearing a cheeky grin. In her hands is an oversized bouquet of pink and purple daisies and lilies and an iced coffee. The arrangement in her hand screams Dexter, mimicking the flowers he got me last time I was *pissed* at him.

"Thanks, Ariel." I stand from my desk and take the flowers and coffee from her. "The one who delivered this didn't hang around, did he?"

I take a quick sip of the Dunkin' Donuts Iced coffee and moan. *Mocha with coconut just how I like it. Damn bastard.*

"Your hunky best friend? No. He said he was in a hurry, but said you were in desperate need of coffee. He's so sweet," she gushes, and I can see the little hearts dancing in her eyes.

"Right, isn't he's the greatest?" Kayleigh pops her head in and Ariel and I both roll our eyes. "Was there anything for me?"

"Why would there be anything for you*?"* Ariel snips narrowing her eyes at her. I've been made well aware I'm not the only one who despises Kayleigh around here.

"Yeah, I thought you guys only had lunch together?" I know he was full of shit about dinner, but I probe anyways, in case I'm wrong.

Cause maybe I really don't know how to read him correctly.

Kayleigh glances away from us and plays with the strands of her hair. "It was, but we had fun. I guess I hoped, that's all. He said we would do it again."

"Well, I'm sure he'll call." I pull the note out of the flowers and place it on my desk along with my coffee and hand her the bouquet. "Here, they'll look better on your desk anyway."

"Oh." Her eyes grow large, taking the flowers from me. "Thanks, M."

Ariel rises her eyebrow, asking silently, *'what are you doing?'* I lift my hand and wave her away. I have something I need to do. Something that's been boiling for months. Ariel gives me a stiff nod and scurries away back to the front.

"Kayleigh, before you go put those in water. Can you please do me a favor?" I push back my shoulders, standing taller. Ready to throw down the law and show Miss Thang here who is in charge.

"Um sure?"

"From here on out, I'm going to need you to stop undermining my decisions and messing with every client to make me look bad. It's getting really old and you using my best friend to try and fuck with me was the last straw."

"I don't know what you're talking about." She laughs nervously, looking to the door, her finger curling around her hair…*which drives me positively insane.*

"You don't? Well, I have plenty of examples for you. How about we start with that since you've been gone for the last several days not one thing has gone wrong. No canceled orders. No fuck ups. Then when you came back Thursday, lo and behold, shit hits the fan with your name written all over it. And let's talk about what happened *today.*" My voice rises and I step in closer to her, but she has the nerve to stare at me looking unrepentant, which stirs my frustration more. "Today, I have caterers telling me *you* told them, I told you to tell them to change seafood dishes to steak. And I had floral arrangements being canceled for next week's event. So, do you want to try again to tell me that you don't know what I'm talking about?"

"I did what I had to do," she bites out harshly, but I shake my head confused. She's not making any sense to me.

Had to do what?

"What, why? You have your future set here. Why in the hell do you have to screw me over?"

"Please! Like you *don't* know," she scoffs, crossing her arms over her chest, crinkling the flowers between them.

"No. I don't," I shriek, losing the rest of my cool with this *girl.*

"My future is only set here if I outshine your ass. That's why you were to train me. Make me great and if I

165

can't learn from the best, *well*, he's giving the job to you. And I'm going to be one of your—*lackeys,*" she hisses and pushes her way further into my office.

"That's not true. Everyone knows he's already picked you. You're his niece for Christ sakes."

"Yeah, but you're his star pupil or whatever. He taught you everything he knows. All I heard was all about you and how great you are. I mean there's who else around here, Alberta and JoAnna? Do you really think he was going to pick them to help take over? I tried to screw a couple of things over, so you wouldn't seem so perfect. That way I could stop hearing how wonderful *you are* and how he can't believe how amazing *you are*. *And* you still managed to fix everything!" she screams and throws the flowers down on my desk. Her chest heaves in and out and I think she's about to attack me when she backs to the door. "But you'll fuck up. I know you will. Nobody is perfect."

She's fucking certifiable.

"Or you could let me train you and you could've done good and succeeded?" I question, figuring I'll play the nice route and get this crazy thing out of my office while I can. "God, have you ever thought that maybe running this company isn't what I would want? If you weren't such a…" *Fuck nice, call her like she is Meadow!* "…such a bitch and did your damn job, maybe I wouldn't mind working for you."

"Whatever. We will see what my uncle has to say about all this."

"Go ahead. I don't think I care anymore." I fling my hand dismissing her.

"Well, good," she huffs, flinging her damn hair over

her shoulder, and leaves my office.

My head throbs as I settle into my chair and take a sip of my now half-melted iced coffee. I pick up the note that was attached to my flowers and sigh, not knowing what to make of Dexter's words.

I don't want to lose you.
Forever and ever…remember?
Can we please talk?
I'm sorry, Dex

There's a gentle knock on my door and my head raises from the note to see Mr. Hanson standing there with his arms crossed. "Meadow, can I talk to you for a minute?" I toss Dex's note to my desk as he closes the door and I prep myself for getting reprimanded or fired.

How the hell did Kayleigh get to him so fast?

"Yeah." I give him my best smile and wave my hand to the seat in front of my desk. Instead, he moves closer to me, opting to remain standing firm in front of me.

"I overheard what happened between you and Kayleigh minutes ago."

My face heats and I sink down in my chair. Well, shit. I'm not sure if that's worse than Kayleigh crying to him or not. "Listen, Mr. Hanson, I'm sorry."

"You should be sorry," he states firmly and my eyes drop to my lap, "for not coming to me in the first place about what was going on."

My head pops up and my mouth drops open. "What?"

"Meadow, if something is going on, I would hope you could come to me," he says sincerely. This is a man I have looked up to and admired for many years, but there was no way in hell I was going to tattle on his niece.

"With all due respect, Mr. Hanson, she's your niece. The heir to the company. Nobody around here was going to say anything because it was her word over ours."

He chuckles and perches himself on the edge of my desk. "Yes, I guess I do understand that. I only wish the rumor that she was the heir to the company never started. I'll be perfectly honest, I did hope to leave this company within my family. I never had any kids and Kayleigh was the closest I had to a daughter. I had hoped if she trained under you and me in the next few years, she would learn everything and have the skill to take over. I never thought she would stoop so low and do what she did."

"When I first met her, I didn't expect it either," I chuckle dryly. "I honestly didn't know what to do, but to keep fixing what I could, or to keep working around the problem."

"See, that's what I admire about you, Meadow. You have this drive, no matter how tough things get, you keep going." Inwardly I snort, thinking '*yeah right*.' Maybe at work, but my personal life, not so much. "You know, when I first met you, you had this same spark, and fiery spirit I did when I started out. You were so willing to work, do anything and learn, that by the time you graduated you were past the skills of my two top coordinators here. I trusted my gut with promoting you as fast as I did, and it's worked out well, for this company and for you. Now, I guess since Kayleigh has let the cat out of the bag so to speak, I guess I can share with you my thoughts for when I retire."

The next words out of his mouth shock and amaze

me. It appears little Miss Kayleigh sunshine wasn't lying about Mr. Hanson wanting to give me the company if she couldn't handle her dues. Over the next five years, he wants to train me and eventually make me the CEO of Hanson Event Planners if that's something I want.

How can I say no? And in the meantime, he's also going to give me a raise.

These crappy couple of days now have at least one upside.

"Now, let's talk about my little Angel, Kayleigh." He rubs his hands on his pants and rises off my desk. "If she promises to change, do you think you could give her another chance?"

"Only if she stops messing with my clients. *And* maybe it would be wise if she works with JoAnna or Alberta for a bit."

"I believe that will be a good idea, and I'll talk to her, trust me. But I think she *might be* taking a small break for a while till she gets her act together," he hints, and I only wish that break would be permanent, but I keep my lips zipped. "Kayleigh has always been spoiled, but believe it or not, there is good somewhere in there. I hope after some time away she will come back and you'll be able to see it. I did have great hope if she learned from you, she'd be able to work her way to the top, but—" He shrugs. "What do you say next week we get together and talk some more about all this. Give you a chance to let this all sink in?"

"That sounds like a good idea, Mr. Hanson. Thank you. I can't tell you how much this all means to me." I stand, putting out my hand.

"You've earned it, Meadow." He takes my hand and shakes it. "I only do hope next time you come to me if you have any issues."

"I will. I promise."

He nods and turns to leave my office. I collapse back into my chair, overtaken by the events of today. I pick up my phone, and my thumb hovers over my contact list, wanting to tell Dexter the good news. He's always the first person I tell everything, and now—*Now* I want to be able to tell him, and then afterward he'll pick me up in his arms and kiss me with everything he has.

I can't have that. And it rips me up inside once again.

I throw my phone aside and bury myself in my work, trying to block out the thoughts of everything I can't have and focus on what I do have. At least here at my job, the future is rich and bright.

"He brings forth another gift," Mel chuckles and sits on the edge of the bed holding a yellow package. "I don't get why he doesn't drop it off himself."

"Because he *knows* I don't want to see him yet."

It's been five days since I have, and I admit I miss him—*a lot.* The days aren't the same not seeing his brown eyes, the stubble on his face, his smile and hearing him laugh. But I still ache deep inside my heart, knowing he *can't* love me fully.

Each day he sends me something; the first day was

flowers, the second was my favorite chocolates from this little bakery downtown, and yesterday was a teddy bear that resembled one he got me as a child. They're all sweet and I know they come from his heart, but every time I see one, it gives me this false hope that it could mean more. Instead, there are no words of love or admiration, only that he misses me, or he can't lose me and wants to talk.

I never thought our vow of "forever and ever," that we made when we were eleven would ever be tested like this.

I have to see him on Saturday, and it gives me a little more time to wrap my mind around everything.

Okay, so I really wish he would knock down the door, forget what I would want, and declare his love to me. "What do you think it is today?"

"I don't know. You open it." I tell her and play with the eternity necklace he gave me for my birthday.

"My pleasure." She giggles and rips open the envelope and pulls out a CD. "Ha. The man made you a mix CD. If that doesn't scream love."

"No, we used to make these things all the time when we were kids." I take the disc from her and look over the song list. It has a lot of my favorites, along with a few sappy romantic songs such as Aerosmith's "I Don't Want to Miss a Thing." and "All of Me" by John Legend, but I don't try to make anything of it because those are also songs I like.

"Any note?" I ask.

"No," she says as she double checks the inside of the envelope.

"Hmm. I'm surprised." He attached a note to all the other gifts he left me. Guess he's giving up now.

"Why don't you call him? Put him out of his misery a bit. Maybe tell him you'll talk later?"

"I texted him on Monday and told him thanks." I sigh. "That counts, right?"

"I guess?" She's not convinced, but I don't know what she wants from me. She didn't have her heart stomped all over by a man, and now said man, is sending the worst mixed signals ever.

"I told you. I need to figure out how to get past this hurt. Like there's nothing more I want to do than fix the friendship, and the gifts tell me that's what he wants too…"

"I think they say more."

"I see, *'Meadow you're my best friend, and I can't lose you."* If this was love, then I need action and the actual words. Why not write a card or a banner that says, geez I don't know, 'I love you'. This is nothing different than everyday stuff between us." My hand brushes my necklace again. "This was more of a statement. Hell, maybe I should tell him to stop." I pause and fall to the bed. "It's just how do we go back to trying to be normal again. How do I go on seeing him happy with someone else? How do I stop—loving *loving* him? Like ever?" I collapse to the bed.

It's what's been driving me the craziest.

"Like I even tried to fucking google this shit. I wondered if there was some kind of blog, like a I Fell for My Best Friend: And He Doesn't Love Me, Now What? Or anything like that."

"Did you find anything?" Mel chuckles and falls down beside me.

"Oh yeah, tons. None did much to make me feel any

better. Some left the friendship behind while some continue to fake it and live forever with that pain. I wish I could rewind all of this. I blame Pickles for dying. Maybe I wouldn't have fallen for him so hard then."

"Oh honey," Mel grabs my hand, cracking a smile, "you loved him way long before that rat dog died."

"Don't call him a rat dog!" I defend my poor lost pup.

"I call it like I see it. Anyways, as I was saying, you were in love with him by the time you guys moved into the house. You only *think* it full flamed by the time Pickles died for the both of you. I think maybe when he was dating Molly."

"Ugh, that *bitch,"* I sneer and slam my fist into the mattress. I want to cry again remembering how close I came to losing Dexter because of her and her lies. Mel laughs at my reaction and I'm so glad that she can laugh at it now. I can't. "That is nothing to laugh about."

"No, but she was extra psycho because she was damn jealous of you two. But there was a shift there. You guys got closer when she started fucking with you. When he finally came to your side and believed you, he dumped her. That was the shift. I think. Then again you two were always like the oddest friends on earth. I mean you could run your hand up on his crotch, make the man hard or play kiss, and it might have meant nothing…and it wasn't that, that changed with you two, but it was the looks, the light touches, and the gentle way he took care of you. It's like an inferno that has been building for so long. We all started to see that you two were in love with each other. That's why we were always on your case and his."

"But Molly was two years ago though."

173

"Yeah, and you two have been driving us crazy for a very long time. Like get married already," she groans, knocking me in the shoulder.

"I'm sorry I've been making your life so hard." I laugh and throw a pillow at her head.

I'm settled into a table at my favorite coffee Shoppe on my lunch break. I love it here because they always play the best music from the early nineties and it's quiet. I'm scrolling through my calendar for next week when I smell the familiar scent of lemongrass and rosewood.

"Hey, Meadow." Julian slips into the chair across from me. "How you been?"

"I've been *super*. You?" I mutter sarcastically and bat my eyes as I take a sip of my caramel latte.

"Wow, your answer sounds a lot like someone else I know," he says smugly, and I knock his foot from under the table.

"What do you want?" I sigh, knowing why he's here, ten blocks away from his own office.

"I can't say hi to my friend?"

"I didn't say that," I huff. "I know you have something you want to say. So, say it."

"Fine, you're right, I do have something to say. For the last couple of days, I have my best architect moping around my building, looking like the undead. The only person that could make him come alive again would be you. So, I was kinda hoping, you know—" He waves his hand and I shake my head.

"That what? I'll tell him everything is going to be okay? I mean you're more than welcome to tell him that. It's not a lie. I know your kind of all in the middle of this and I'm sorry for that. I never meant for any of this."

"I know. You don't have to apologize. If it had bothered me, I wouldn't have played along. Anyways, he doesn't know I'm here. On Saturday he came to see me. He told me everything that happened. I won't tell you everything he said to me. I do believe he needs to tell you what is going through his mind because I wouldn't explain it right."

"But he told *you*." I cut him off. "I'm the one person who he should have explained it to that day. We used to share everything. I'm the one person who would understand." *Especially, when it comes to Wes. That kills me the most. "*Instead, he assumed I wouldn't get it. That hurts. He's sent me gifts, notes, voicemails, and still nothing of what the hell he's *thinking*. I need…time."

Though, I'm not sure how much time that is. Because I do miss him. I feel so defeated and most of all lost and confused.

"I understand, Meadow. I do." He reaches over and takes my shaky hand. "I didn't mean to upset you. I think he told me because I was safe and not so close to what you guys went through. It's not that he wants to keep you in the dark about what happened. I'm sure he will be telling you soon. He's terrified, but Meadow, he does love you."

"You know everyone keeps saying that. I'm finding

it hard to believe."

How can I believe it? He's not the one in front of me now confessing the words.

I want everything back to the way it used to be. I want my best friend back and never want to have to worry about things being awkward between us. Though I feel it will always be because no matter how much I try, I can't stop loving him.

.

Chapter Twelve

Dexter

The days have drawn on since I've seen Meadow, and I'm going insane. I can't eat because my stomach is in a permanent knot in the aftermath. I can't sleep because every time I close my eyes, I see that broken look in her eyes when I couldn't tell her I loved her back.

I knew I could've easily solved all my issues and gone to Mel's, or her job, and forced my way to see her if I wanted to. It's just I needed to work out my shit, first. I had to deal with that night of Wes death, to be able to let it go—to confess what felt like my biggest sin. And the first place I had to start was with—well, Wes.

Though now as I sit in the grassy field, in front of Wes' headstone I feel ridiculous about 'asking' him permission to date 'his' girl. This grief counselor I talked to the other day thought it would be good for me to talk to my friend and maybe it would give me some worldly answers. That somehow Wes would answer me beyond the grave with a sign. *Okay,* it's not what he said, but it's what it felt like. I've never been one to pray, not even after his death, so here goes nothing.

"Hey, buddy, I have no idea what I'm doing and if you can see me, I bet you could see how much of an idiot I look like right now. Well, I guess maybe you can. I don't know how all this afterlife stuff works. Meadow is convinced that you're always there watching over us, which honestly gives me the creeps, especially with what I'm about to tell you. But if what she says is true, then you already know." I rub my forehead feeling like a dumbass. "But first I have to tell you how sorry I am, man, for that night. I wish I had listened to you. You were always the one who had his head on straight and knew better for both of us. If I didn't want to be such an ass and practically want your girl for myself, you would still be here. There's not a day that goes by that I don't miss you, Wes. Meadow does too. You know despite her wanting me now." I chuckle, looking towards the sky, waiting for something to drop out of it for being a cocky ass in this moment.

I mean, I did come here looking for a sign. It would be my luck that's the one I get.

"But seriously, she does miss you, and I hate it so much that I can never see how great you two would have been. I'll be forever sorry, and I hope you can forgive me. And I guess I'm here because I need to forgive myself and to tell you that I do love her. Like, I get why you fell for her while I was still thinking the thought of kissing her was gross. Now, I get it. She's amazing. She's everything I've always wanted and never knew I wanted, hiding right in plain sight this whole time. Like I really do love her, Wes. I do. I know you wanted me to take care of her, but I bet you didn't expect me to fall in love with her, right? I bet you want to kick my ass, huh?" I chuckle.

My laugh is met with a light feminine one that startles the shit out of me. With my hand over my racing heart, my head snaps behind me, to see my Aunt Martha standing there with a bouquet of orange and yellow flowers.

"I highly doubt he would want to kick your butt."

"You scared me," I tell her, as I get my breathing back to normal.

"I'm sorry. I shouldn't have interrupted, but it sounded like you needed to hear it." She gives me a warm smile and kneels next to me, laying the colorful arrangement down.

"I wasn't expecting anybody to stop by today, I mean—"

She places her hand on my knee, stopping me. "I wasn't going to, but then I felt like coming to say hi to my baby boy." Martha looks towards his headstone, then back at me. "Maybe now I know why I had the urge."

Ah, so is this my sign?

"Wesley would have wanted nothing more than for you and Meadow to be happy."

"I know."

"Do you?" She taps my knee, and I shrug. "I've been talking to your mom and Valerie a bit lately. They said something happened between you and Meadow and think maybe it's because you've been holding onto your feelings for her. Your mom thinks it had something to do with my son?"

My eyes close and I groan. Nothing is ever safe from those women. "Do you three just get together and drink tea and talk about our lives?"

"No." She pauses, and I raise an eyebrow at her. "We

drink wine. You're our children, we're supposed to talk about you. But I'm so glad to hear you admit that you're in love with Meadow. It's about time. And if anyone could love Meadow more than my son, it's you, Dexter Greene. You know, Wes told me something once, that maybe I should've told you sooner when I saw yours and Meadow's feelings start to change." She grabs my hand, and the only thing I can think is, how the fuck did everyone see this shit but me?

"Wes had always known that somewhere deep down you loved Meadow more than just a friend." My mouth opens and she holds her hand up, stopping me from talking, but I'm blown away by this revelation. "Now, he knew you would never cross the line and he was never jealous or worried about it. He trusted you, don't get me wrong. Get the panicked, horrid look off your face, young man, and let me finish." My Aunt laughs, bopping me on the nose much like she always did when I was a little kid.

"It's hard to believe that he ever thought that about me."

"It wasn't in a bad way. I'm not telling you this to upset you. I'm telling you this because it's why Wes admired you so much and looked up to you even though you were so much younger."

"Okay, now you have me confused."

"Because whether you might know it or not, the second Wes admitted that he was in love with Meadow, you put whatever feelings you had for her away. Even after he passed you still honored his love for her, am I right on that?" I nod. "It's time, hun. It's time to let it go. He would want this because he would want you and her happy. And he'd much rather see her with you than some other bozo. Remember that one guy she brought home? Sonto or something?"

"Santino," I laugh. "Yeah. Wes would have killed me beyond the grave if I let her keep that one around."

"See." She smacks my leg. "That's why you are the better choice for her, and Wes would want it, no matter what."

"I miss him," I say softly, looking back at the gravestone.

"I do too, every day." She pulls me into a tight hug. When she pulls away, she places her hand on my cheek. "Just promise me you won't be afraid to love her, son, especially now. And you know what, it would be nice to have some babies in this family. You and Meadow are the only options."

"Whoa, whoa, whoa. Aunt Martha…slow down. Let me tell her I love her first. Babies are like *wayyy* way down the road." My heart rate spikes once again and my head shakes wildly.

She laughs and wraps me back in her arms. "Oh, Dexter, there's nothing better than seeing you panic."

"This is quite the party you all have set up." Randy smacks my shoulder as I finish putting together the rest of the decorations.

I got here early to help under my mother's duress thinking things weren't going to get done. I came rushing over to *help,* thinking Meadow would be here also lending a hand. She wasn't. She's dealing with the cake and the caterers.

Figures I was fucking stuck hanging streamers and blowing up balloons alone.

"Have you and Meadow kissed and made up yet?" Julian snickers. I'm glad the asshole finds it so fucking funny.

"No, because your plan sucked." I toss one of the deflated balloons at him.

"I told you I knew nothing." He raises his hands. "*And* it was mostly all your ideas if I remember right. I also ran into her yesterday and put in a good word for you. Maybe she'll come around today."

"She has no choice but to come around today, fucker. But if anyone can ignore someone she doesn't want to talk to, it's Meadow."

"Listen, you're in the dog house, and all you can do to get out of it is to keep begging till your knees bleed man." Randy chuckles, grabbing one of the loose balloons.

"Thanks, what a way to make me feel better."

"No problem. Plus, no matter how much she wants to avoid you, she won't be able to. You're sitting next to her. Be sure to be on your game," Randy reminds me, and that's about the only good thing I have going for me tonight.

"And tell her you love her, or I fucking swear, man, I will fucking drop kick you from here to Bakersfield," Julian adds picking up his bottle of water from the table.

"I will. I will." I wave them off and walk away. I'm in need of a beer and a place to hide from my mother before she finds me something else to do.

The open bar isn't open yet, so I wander outside the dining hall for some fresh air. It does nothing to help with the jitters about seeing Meadow soon, so I start to pace the sidewalk.

I miss her like crazy.

I thought about telling her every time I picked up the phone, or every note I wrote that I loved her, but it never felt right not doing it in person. Here I thought I knew how to woo Meadow Lexington. I sent her all the things I knew she would like, all the things from when we were kids. I had hoped they would show her how I felt or that she would at least come to me and we could talk.

But I was wrong, so fucking wrong.

A car door slams, grabbing my attention and I see Meadow stepping out of her Terrain.

I haven't seen her in a week, and I find myself gaping at her like I haven't seen her in years, lost in how amazing she looks in a strapless pale pink dress. Her auburn hair is curled and flowing down her shoulders. It's been so long since I've seen her so done up.

I wonder if this is what a groom feels like on their wedding day.

Her eyes lift to mine and she gives me a weak smile as she keeps walking. That's when I realize I haven't moved and I'm about to blow my chance.

Unsticking my feet, I dash to her, blocking her path. "Hey."

"Hi." She tries to dart around me, but I grab her shoulders. "Dexter, let me go."

"Can we talk, please," I beg.

She sighs, and her head drops. "Alright. You have one minute."

"I miss you. I miss my best friend. It's been so hard to come home to that house and know you won't be there."

"I miss you too, but…"

"Haven't you been getting the things I've sent you?" I interrupt her not wanting to know what her *but* could be.

"I have, but can you stop?"

"Why?"

"Because you're making this all harder." Her voice breaks and she grips the eternity necklace I gave her. *At least that still means something to her.* "We will get through this. Our friendship will be okay. I need time to accept that you can't love me like that and know that it's okay. That it doesn't matter. And you sending me gifts and stuff doesn't help right now."

"Meadow…that's not why."

"Then why?" she whimpers, holding in the tears welling in her eyes. It kills me inside to know that me being in denial for so long has done this to her. "To say sorry? I don't need you to do that either. I get it, Dex. It's fine. If I could, I would take it all back and wish we never slept together or admitted that I loved you more than a friend. Then maybe we wouldn't be here right now with all this hurt and wondering where our friendship stands. That kills me the most. I don't know, but give me time, and I'm sorry too if this hurts you that I can't talk to you. I wish I didn't do what I did, but ugh!" She lets out a frustrated scream and a tear slips from her eye. "I can't do this right now. I can't even look at you without it all still hurting…I'm sorry." She pushes by me and runs inside.

Now I feel like a bigger shit for what I did. Her fucking birthday is gonna haunt me more than Wes' death.

No matter how much I tried to remember that night, it's a total wash.

My mother comes up the sidewalk and she eyes me curiously, placing her hand on my arm. "Dexter? Everything okay?"

"If I said yes, would you believe me?"

"No. What's going on?"

I sigh, knowing there's no hiding from my mother. "I've been doing all these things to show her what I feel about her, and she still won't talk to me. I thought she would see that I do want her, that I do love her, and she thinks I'm only trying to save the friendship."

"Have you actually said the words, Dexter?"

"No," I mutter.

"Why not?"

"Because I wanted to say them to her face. And have her know I mean I actually *love* her. She's so upset right now, and I don't think she would hear me even if I did."

"Well, if there's anything we all learned over the years there's no time to waste. Every second is valuable, dear."

"I know, but you saw her, she can't even look at me."

"Maybe you need to make more of a grand gesture. One she won't be able to look away from."

"You mean besides grabbing her and throwing her over my shoulder like a caveman?"

"Yes, besides that. Leave it to your mother. I might have an idea. Did you ever finish your speech?"

"No?" It's been the last thing on my mind. I figured

I could wing it or say ditto to whatever Meadow says. That's probably what they all expected me to do anyway.

"I didn't think so," she laughs, proving my point. "Which works in your favor because you're going to need this to come from your heart. Oh, and I happened to have talked to Martha."

"Oh, Jesus…"

"If this doesn't get you out of the dog house. I don't know what will," Randy snickers patting me on the back.

I told the guys my plan, well my mother's and Aunt's plan mostly, and after they gave me a hard time and called me every sissy name in the book, they wished me luck. I was going to need it. This feels like my only chance to do it right.

I make my way to the stage and pick up the mic. Tapping it twice the feedback feeds into the speakers, grabbing everyone's attention. My eyes shift around the crowd looking for the most beautiful girl in the room, praying she'll finally look at me.

When I find her, she's gathered around Mel and Steph. Steph is whispering furiously in her ear and Meadow's brushing her away.

"How's everyone doing tonight? If you don't know already, I'm Dexter Greene. Frank and Martha's nephew.

I was supposed to do this great speech earlier, but instead, I figured it might fit better now getting the karaoke portion of the night started. Because if there's one thing my Uncle Frank and Aunt Martha taught me, it's never a party without karaoke. Almost every Saturday night since I could remember they would have people over and they would have set up the karaoke machine. Their son, Wes, Meadow, and I would stay up way past our bedtimes to watch their friends and our parents make asses of themselves ruining some great classic songs. Uncle Frank, I'm sorry, but Journey was never the same."

"Hey, now! I remember lots of request for encores," he yells out and everyone laughs.

"That was only cause we wanted to stay up longer," I call back. *And we might have been distracting him and sneaking beers the older we got.* "So, I would like to start the karaoke portion of the night not only dedicating this song to Frank and Martha, but also someone extremely special to me. Someone I hope I can spend thirty-five years loving just as long and hard as my Aunt and Uncle do each other."

Finally, Meadow's eyes meet mine, but they're bugged out in what appears a state of utter shock.

"It should be pretty easy though, I have already spent about twenty-four years with her, and we've haven't killed each other *yet.* Though there have been some close calls."

Now, most of the guests' eyes have glinted towards Meadow and I can hear her name also being murmured through the crowd.

"The song I picked is from Aunt Martha's favorite band and she loved them so much it became Wesley's standby band to always sing and purposely ruin to drive her crazy. But he admitted to me once he actually liked *all* their music, Aunt Martha."

She giggles and nods, wiping a lone tear from her cheek. "I always knew. He was a terrible liar like someone else I know."

"So, there's no doubt I had to pick a song from their collection. Now this song might not necessarily express everything I want to say, but it says a lot that I want to say to her. Meadow Lexington, this is for you."

The chords of Chicago's "Hard to Say I'm Sorry" start and though I've done karaoke a million times, I usually have had a couple of shots to calm the nerves.

But nope, I thought I needed to be sober for this, so she'd take me seriously.

Now I'm sweating bullets because watching Meadow as I go into the chorus her body is shaking as she cries. Mel and Steph try to comfort her and I'm not understanding her reaction at all. I go to walk up to her, and she shakes her head at me. Even Mel and Steph look at me confused, and I pause my steps not knowing what to do now and feel like an idiot.

Thankfully, as I check out the crowd around me, they don't seem to have noticed her hesitation towards me and have taken up slow dancing along with my aunt and uncle.

Thank God for small miracles.

By the time I get to the lyrics saying I want to make it up to her, she breaks out of Mel and Steph's hold and runs towards the back doors. Both girls shrug, unsure of what happened, and I'm stuck to the end of this damn song.

Once it ends, I hand the mic to my mother and chase after my girl.

Racing out the double doors of the hall, I head for the parking lot thinking she's taking off. When I spot her car and her not in it, I begin to panic wondering where she could've gone.

How far could she have gotten in that dress and in those heels?

"Meadow?" I yell, running towards the back of the building. I call for her again but feel like a moron knowing she won't answer me back even if she can hear me. I spot a bridge that leads out to a lake and in the distance I see her standing there and looking out to the water. As I approach her she has her arms wrapped protectively around herself. The wind blows back her auburn hair as the setting sun kisses her skin.

She's got her guard up, telling me to back off, and I can make out the tear stains on her cheeks from here, but I've never seen her look more beautiful than in this moment. I'm desperate to take her in my arms and kiss away all of her pain and crumble down that damn wall she has up once and for all.

Tell her again Dex, till she hears you.

Chapter Thirteen

Meadow

"You need to come with us." Mel tugs on my arm and pulls me to the middle of the dance floor where everyone is starting to gather around for karaoke.

"If this is to sing. I'm not really in the mood."

"No, we're not singing, but somebody else is. I think it'll be great." Steph grins, linking her arm with mine.

My first thought is Frank is about to serenade Martha with a possible rendition of "My Girl," but when I see Dexter take the stage, I know this can't be good.

"Oh, no." I go to turn away and Mel and Steph hold onto me harder as Dex taps into the mic drawing everyone's attention.

"You two need to talk," Steph whispers loudly in my ear. "You can't avoid him forever." I wave her off. Not wanting to listen to the truth.

I have been avoiding him all night. I didn't even sit next to him at dinner, changing tables to sit with our friends instead. Even though I feel like a bitch for doing so, my heart is not able to take seeing him. I know a part of me should hear him out, but I let my fear win. Everything inside me still aches with the thought of us never being together. The second I came face to face with him for the first time all week, the stabbing, heartbreaking pain returned, and I fled.

Much like I want to do now.

I do admit he looks broken and I might've only twisted the knife in his own gaping wound when I told him I wish I never loved him more than a friend. But I did at that second wish I could've gone back to faking it so I could have my best friend back, the way we used to be before everything got so complicated.

"So, I would like to start the karaoke portion of the night, not only dedicating this song to Frank and Martha, but also to someone extremely special to me. Someone I hope I can spend thirty-five years loving just as long and hard as my Aunt and Uncle do each other."

My eyes meet Dexter's and widen in disbelief at his words. My body trembles as he says the words I have been longing to hear, but are they *the* words. I feel everyone's eyes on me and hear my name muttered through the crowd as Dexter carries on with his speech.

Then when he starts to sing, and though his voice is like smooth honey, making my insides swoon, his song selection only further baffles me.

Why is he doing this?

Why can't he give it to me straight and save me the headache if he wants to only say sorry or I love you?

Beside me, Mel and Steph are trying to grab my attention, but my heart is thumping wildly in my chest and next thing I know I'm crying. Dexter takes a step forward, gravitating my way. His eyes are locked on mine. There's a longing, and a look of sadness shining in them. It's as if he's asking me, begging me to listen to this, and run into his arms and forgive him. But there's still so much to talk about, so much to say. Instead, I'm consumed with my hurt again and signal for him not to come closer. Unable to take any more, I break free from Mel and Steph's hold and run for the back door—away from my fear. Away from all this pain.

A cool breeze hits my face as I bust out the doors of the banquet hall. The fresh air does nothing to cool my anxiety from my racing thoughts. I swear I can still hear the chords of Chicago and Dexter's voice shifting through the air as I wander off for a place to think, but I'm sure it's all in my head.

I'm all confused and conflicted, my mind circling around and around to the point it might blow. He tells me he loves me, all I've wanted, but where has this been?

Is it even true or is he going to take it back again like at my birthday and tell me he can't?

If this is a change, then why hasn't he banged down the door and told me sooner? Or is it my fault for not calling when he knew I needed space?

Why is love so fucking confusing?

I'm about to scream into the sky, cursing the gods for making everything so complicated when I catch him out of the corner of my eye. He's watching me, shifting on his feet with his hands stuffed in his pocket.

Alright, let's do this.

Taking a steady breath, I spin around to face him and cross my arms over my chest. "What do you want, Dexter?"

"Why did you run off?"

Erica Marselas

"Because you're sending the most confusing signals ever. What do you want from me, Dexter? Because I don't think my heart can take much more from you right now. Being told one thing and then being told another. I don't think I can do it."

"I love you, Meadow. I honest to God love you, love you. The hearts and flowers kind. The kind where I want to spend kissing your lips forever. The love that makes me want to spend forever with you and never let you go."

"What happened to you not deserving me? And that you *couldn't* cause of Wes? Huh? You sure as hell didn't feel this way all week or you would have come to see me and just told me you loved me, instead of all *this*. Saved me from all this damn hurt." My voice cracks and every muscle in my already achy heart clenches wondering what could have been so life-affirming. Could this really have been a change or is he only saying this because he misses me and doesn't know what else to do?

"You're right. I should've said all of it to you a long time ago. I sent you the gifts, with every intention of telling you I loved you, but it felt wrong not saying it you in person. You deserved that. And I also knew you needed time. I guess maybe also, I only knew how to say it fully on your birthday…" He gives me a half smile and I roll my eyes. "Listen, there's something I have to tell you. And I'm not sure how you're going to take it. It's about Wes and that night."

"What?"

He looks to the ground and scratches the back of his head. When he finally looks back at me, I can see the pain and regret clouding his brown eyes. "Your gonna laugh, but it was Julian who started making me see my errors and

194

I did find someone else to talk to about this."

"Dex, what are you talking about?" I step closer to him, my hand reaching out to touch his shoulder. The urge to wrap him in my arms is great. I know whatever this is, it's huge, and weighing him down, but I wait and squeeze his shoulder, a sign that I'm here for him, no matter what.

"That night, Wes and I were fighting. Wes didn't want me to take you to that party because he knew we were going to drink. I wanted to hang out with you, without him for once, without you guys dry fucking humping. Like you were selfishly my friend first. I don't know. He was all Mr. Responsibility all of a sudden. But I took you. We got drunk. We had so much fun." His face falls and his brown eyes well with tears. "I only wish I knew it wouldn't have been worth it. I think you were even asleep by the time Wes came to pick us up. You didn't even budge when we fought on the way back."

"He didn't want you to take me to that party?" I shake my head and can't fathom any reason why Wes would have stopped me besides it being so far away. "You know, if it makes you feel better, I might have made you take me if he told me no too."

I have no clue if it's true. But damn, Dex and I didn't do good at being told 'no' when we were teenagers.

"Not really, Meadow. Because I was trying to be a dick. When he picked us up, I wanted to be like '*fuck you, I took Meadow out and you couldn't stop me.*' It was so fucking childish. But I never got to see you anymore. Then what does karma do?" He takes a shaky breath and runs his hands through his now messy hair. "That's why it always felt wrong to have feelings for you because I took away Wes from you and you from him. All because I was being a selfish fucking prick. If we got together then I felt I was being selfish all over again. Stealing you away from him. I could never take his place because I don't deserve it. I'm sorry, Meadow."

Now I do grab him and pull him into my arms, squeezing him so tight I never *want* let go. "Dex, it's not your fault. You didn't ask that drunk to hit us."

"I think I'm finally getting that now…but it's been so fucking hard not to feel that." He breathes and wraps me tightly back. "I made sure if I did anything right, it was I did everything I could to live by his last words."

"To take care of me?" I pull back a little to look at his face and he nods. I sniff back the tears remembering Dexter curling up beside me in my hospital bed after the accident telling me Wes' final words. "You've been doing an *okay* job at that," I tease. He's been doing better than okay. Dexter has been like my savior, and sometimes my white knight.

"Thanks," he scoffs, and I'm glad to be able to make a tiny smile appear on his face, if only for a second.

"I only wish you trusted me with this. You really think I would have been mad or even hated you?"

"I don't know. You loved him. I mean I loved the man too. But you two, I think would've been forever. You spent weeks and weeks not being able to get out of bed. You wouldn't eat, and I think you must have lost fifteen pounds. You were depressed for a long time, Meadow, and I thought if I told you, I guess I didn't want to risk losing you too."

"I get it. I do. You want to know something? When I first fell in love with you, I felt guilty too."

His eyes squint curiously. "You did?"

"Yeah. You don't think I don't wonder what life would have been like if Wes was still here? It creeps in my mind once in a while and it breaks my heart. I can't lie and say I don't miss him because I do. But the thing is, he's not here anymore, and I have worked through it. He's not coming back, and I know Wes would want me happy, and he would want you happy. And most of all he would want *us* happy. But god damn if there isn't a part of me where it doesn't kill me to know if Wes was here, I could never have a future with you, because I've fallen so damn hard in love with you. Now maybe it wouldn't have happened if he was alive, but god damn does it hurt to know that I couldn't have you now. And if you're holding onto this guilt because you think he or I or anybody will be mad, you need to let it go. Fully."

"I'm getting there."

"Good." I brush my fingers through his stubbly beard. "Do you think you *can* say those words again."

"I think I can," he smirks but doesn't continue.

I shove his shoulder and he laughs. "Don't mess with me right now."

"Wouldn't dream of it." He grabs my chin, his lips inches from mine. "I love you, so fucking much, Meadow Jane Lexington."

Excitement and pure elation fill my belly. The fear and confusion that was tangled in there from earlier vanishes because there's definitely no denying now the words he is saying are nothing but true.

He *can* love me.

Finally! Damn it!

"I love you, too. So damn much, Dexter William Greene." My fingers curl in his hair as his lips touch mine.

197

His tongue swirls with mine, and my skin ignites under his touch. I can feel every ounce of his love for me conveyed through this one earth-shattering, desperate, longing kiss. In return, I'm giving back that same fire and desire, the one that's been burning in my belly *for God knows* how long now.

He grabs my ass, pulling me closer, his erection stabbing me in the belly. I moan against him, sweet memories of my birthday coming to the forefront, wanting nothing more than to repeat it all again. This time, Dex would be throwing me down to the grass, having his way with me despite all the people inside.

"Meadow?" He breathes, pulling back from me. A smug grin spreads across his face. "You know, I might have always thought I couldn't have you. But believe it or not, I don't think my dick ever played in on that game." He pokes his rigid cock into me. I wet my lips, recounting all the fond memories of all the times I drove him crazy. Sometimes as simple as one touch. "*He* always knew what he wanted with you."

"So for the first time, you might have been listening to the wrong head."

"I think so."

"Wow." I giggle, now realizing how ridiculous, yet accurate, the conversation is. "I don't think that was something I ever thought I would ever say."

He leans back into me and wraps a strand of my hair around his finger. "I'm definitely going to listen to *him* now. Because all I want to do is take this dress off you and ravish the fuck out of you."

Our lips are millimeters apart from each other when there's an unsynchronized clearing of a couple of throats.

I break away from Dex, but he keeps me close to him. Pressing his erection into me. I'm sure for our mothers not to get a lookie.

"Did you two happen to forget where you are?" Joy asks, her eyes darting between us.

"We might have been caught up in the moment," Dexter says smugly, looking down at me.

"As much as we are thankful you two love birds have finally gotten through your stubborn heads that you love each other, there have been some requests for an encore."

"Actually, do you think we could head out?" Dex smirks, his eyes dance mischievously. My cheeks heat instantly thinking of the dirty things I want to do to him.

Both our mothers raise their eyebrows and cross their arms. Obviously, they spent too much time over the years punishing us together. "No. Definitely not to do *that.* You're still our kids. Get back inside," Joy says, pointing back towards the ballroom. My mom nods in agreement.

"We weren't going to do *that*," Dex quickly defends. "You have such a dirty mind, *Mother*. We have to move her stuff back into the house. She ran away to Mel's, remember?"

"*Uh-huh,*" my mother retorts sarcastically, "Well, you can do that after the party. It's only a few clothes, not her entire life. Nice try though."

"Isn't this what you guys wanted? Why are you breaking this up again?" Dex grabs my hand, pulling me towards the hall. On the outside, I'm laughing, but on the inside, I'm pouting and stomping my feet just as hard as Dexter right now.

"Because we *live* to make your life complicated. Another song and then pictures, and then some dancing.

Then you can go. Teach you not to be so stubborn, mister," Joy heckles behind us, and I wouldn't expect any less from them.

When Dex and I pass through the double doors, he swings me into his arms bridal style. I squeal so loud in the process, it echoes out into the hall, calling everyone's attention.

"I got her!" Dex shouts out, and everyone cheers, while my face reddens in embarrassment.

"About damn time," Steve and Uncle Frank yell together through the applause and then high five each other. Waves of laughter circle through the cheering crowd.

"Can you put me down now?" I giggle nervously and rest my head to his.

"What? You don't like all the attention? All the eyes on you?" he teases, and I know this has to do with me walking out on him in the middle of his song.

"Actually, I do." I grab his face and press my lips to his, to finish what we started outside. The cheers turn to hoots, but our kiss is quickly broken up by our mothers...*again.*

After a few more rounds of karaoke, where at one-point Frank and Martha do a powerful, moving rendition of "I've Had the Time of My Life," everyone moves to the dance floor.

I fling my arms around Dexter's shoulders and we sway to the music. This party turned out well from the decorations to food to the music. Seeing the happy faces and the beauty of the party is the number one reason I love my job. It makes all the painstaking planning worth it in the end.

Well, except all the shit with Kayleigh in the past. Which reminds me that I haven't told Dexter my news.

"I think I may owe you for the whole Kayleigh thing," I blurt out and his eyes squint looking at me funny.

"Why?"

"Because I think it finally gave me the strength and the courage to stand up to her. She ended up confessing to me that she had been trying to fuck me over, and Mr. Hanson overheard it all. Well, let's say in the next however many years, when he retires, he's going to hand over the company to me if I want it."

"Meadow, that's amazing. I'm so proud of you." He places a light kiss on my lips.

"Thank you. It's crazy. It was the last thing I ever expected. It's still years away and I still have things to learn, but I'm getting a pay raise too."

"Is Kayleigh going to be there still or is she gone now?"

"She's going to be taking some time off, and as long as she has her act together when she comes back, she'll stay. Hopefully, she won't be so bad the second time around, and you and her stay away from each other." I smirk.

"I think I have learned my lesson." He grabs my chin and captures my lips with his. Our tongues dance together as our feet stop.

"You know, I don't think we thought this all the way through," Mel's voice chimes in beside me, but I ignore her and continue losing myself in my man.

"What's that?" Julian perks up.

"We will have to continuously watch them do *that* now, instead of making googly eyes at each other and daydreaming." Dex breaks away from me and shoots Mel a glare, which only makes her laugh. "Don't glare at me, pretty boy. I'm saying we're happy for you. It's going to take a while to get used to the change of scenery."

"Honestly, they look the same to me." Julian chuckles and then spins her around on the dance floor.

"Are you two done now?" Dex asks them, pinching his nose.

"For now." Mel winks before dragging Julian away.

Sometimes I can't *with her.*

Dex pulls me tighter into his chest and his fingers run down my bareback. "Maybe we should sneak away to some closet or something. Spare everyone's eyes." His eyebrows wiggle and his brown eyes gleam wickedly.

"As exciting as that all sounds. We are *not* doing it for the second time, well the first time you remember—sober—in some coat closet. I *do* deserve better than that."

He chuckles. "You're right, you do." He brushes the back of his hand down my cheek. "When we get home, I promise it's going to be perfect."

Home? Home is still hours away. No, that's not going to work.

I grab his tie, saying fuck it. I need him now. We can have *perfect* later. "*But* I wouldn't mind breaking in the backseat of your truck."

"Oh, thank god."

Dexter

"We need to be quick before anybody spots us leaving," I tell her as I check our surroundings. For now, it appears no one is paying us any attention and our bloodhound mothers are off on the other side of the ballroom.

I take her hand and pull her through the crowd to the doors. She's laughing carefree as she stumbles on her heels a bit to keep up with me. We make it safely out the doors without alerting any of the parental units or our crazy friends.

Once to my truck, I push her up against the doors and devour her lips, doing everything in my power not to rip the dress from her body. I don't think I have ever wanted someone so much in my entire life as I want Meadow right now. Her tiny little whimpers against my lips are driving me insane.

"I love you, Meadow. And I'm sorry it took so long ...because god damn…" I grind myself into her, moving my mouth to the side of her neck.

She tastes so damn sweet.

"I love you too but get me in this truck. Now."

I struggle to get the keys out of my pocket because I can't force myself to detach my mouth from Meadow's skin.

"Hurry," she begs. "I'm so wet and I want you so bad, Dex."

Well, fuck! I don't need to be told twice.

Managing to pull myself away from her, I get the

doors open on my Dodge and we pile in the back seat. She kicks her heels off and then bunches her dress up around her hips.

"These are hot." I trace my finger along her slit, that's covered by a pink lace thong.

She wasn't lying. She is soaked.

I'm one lucky son of a bitch.

"Yeah?" she asks, as she shimmies them down her legs. "I'm just glad you won't be able to rip them to shreds like you did on my birthday."

"I ripped them, huh? Nice." I grin while nodding my approval and she throws her panties at my head.

"Shut up."

I shove the lacy garments into my pocket and then proceed to undo my pants, freeing my achy cock from its confines. "Get over here, you." I grab her arm and yank her to me.

"I can't believe we're doing this," she giggles as she maneuvers herself to straddle my lap.

"It was your idea." I pull the bodice of her dress down, exposing her perfect breasts.

"Yeah, but we're taking a huge risk if we get caught."

"As long as it's not the cops, we should be good. Plus, it's our mom's fault for not letting us leave."

I place her breast in my mouth and suck and nip at her cherry colored nipples. She squirms in my lap, begging for more, as I play with them, making them both long and hard.

These are mine. Forever and ever.

"Your perfection, Meadow."

"You're not so bad yourself."

She grips my dick, and runs it along her slick slit,

teasing me, as her sweet juices cover the tip. "Is this what you want?"

"Fuck, baby. I think that's a bit of a no-brainer." My hand slips around the back of her neck, bringing her down to me, needing to consume her lips once more. Feeling I might never get enough of her—ever.

Slowly, she sinks herself onto me, and I groan. The tightness and her silkiness is the heaven I had imagined these last few weeks.

And this reality is better than any fucking wet dream I could ever have.

I could seriously kick myself for waiting so long to have this.

"Darn it," she exclaims with a little giggle.

"What?" I break away from her, eyeing her curiously.

"I was kind of hoping once you got inside of me, it would jump start your memory and you'd remember making love to me on my birthday."

I chuckle and thrust my hips upwards making her yelp. "No, but I'm about to make this memorable for the both of us for always."

"Oh yeah? Is that a threat?" she pants, resting her forehead to mine, as she starts to roll her hips along with my thrusts.

"No, it's a promise. And I'll tell you right now, I'll never forget again."

Chapter Fourteen

Meadow

I lean back in my chair and chew on the edge of my pen, the memories of the special weekend Dexter and I had together flood my mind. We've been together for a month now, and we celebrated by going to North Beach. The relaxation, sunshine, and most of all the great sex is not only what I needed to recharge, but to feel like a brand-new woman. My whole-body tingles and throbs remembering the new heights Dexter took my body to. The sensual massages, the kisses, and how he cherished every inch of me. He made me fall in love *love* with him all over again.

Sure, the walks on the beach, the daiquiris and laying in the sun were nice too. But that man's tongue and fingers are like heaven.

There's a knock on my door, pulling me from my daydream. I throw my pen down to my desk and pretend to look busy before I answer. "Yeah?"

The door opens slowly and Dexter's head pops in around it. "How's my favorite girl?" I smile seeing him.

He steps into my office fully, holding a plastic bag with a yellow smiley face on it. The smell of chicken and ginger fill my office.

"Hey, I wasn't expecting you." I stand from my desk and greet my deliciously sinful boyfriend. *Boyfriend.* Wow. It still boggles my mind sometimes when I think that word.

"I bought us lunch from your favorite Chinese restaurant down the street. Thought you might be hungry." He smirks and kicks the door closed behind him.

"You have no idea." I grab his black skinny tie and roll it around my hand. "I've worked up quite an insatiable appetite after this weekend," I purr, laying a kiss to his jaw.

He lays the bag of takeout on my desk and places his hands on my hips.

"I love you," he whispers, laying little kisses into the side of my neck.

Ever since he uttered those meaningful words at the party, it's as if they took on a whole other life. They became powerful little shocks of electricity, that zipped and zapped every time they left our lips right into our hearts. Maybe it's over dramatic and Hallmark cliché in a way, but when you have loved someone for their whole life, it becomes richer and more significant and your heart does start beating a whole new rhythm.

"Have I told you how much I love hearing that?"

"You're never going to stop hearing it, cause I love telling you."

"Dexter Greene, so mushy." I giggle and he brushes his nose with mine giving me a devilish smile in return.

Oh, I love this look. This look means I'm in trouble.

The good kind of trouble.

The temperature in the room instantly rises, my cheeks and chest flush. I'm now needy and have the urge to touch him. I reach up and run my fingers through his soft hair and plant a kiss to the corner of his lips.

"Do you have any clients coming in or meetings today?"

"No." I bite my lip.

"Mr. Hanson around?" His eyes dance with mine as he undoes the top button of my blouse.

"Nope."

"Good." He leans in and kisses behind my ear. "Because I didn't only come here for lunch."

"I didn't think you did," I whisper and every inch of my skin heats in anticipation.

He hikes up my skirt to my ass, then slides his hands under the rumpled fabric, grabbing ahold of my panties. "You won't be needing these." With the combination of his husky voice and his lustful stare, I'm surprised my thong doesn't melt in his hand.

"No?"

"I should have told you not to even bother wearing them today." He falls to his knees, pulling the thin fabric down my legs. I kick off my heels to free my panties and he stuffs the garment in his pocket.

He spreads my legs and his eyes glint to mine with a delicious threat. "You want me to eat this little…"

"Shut up…" I grab the back of his head and push it into my core. His hands grab my ass, pulling me in closer and he devours me. I throw my head back as he works his magic tongue and it takes me back to yesterday on the beach, as he took me to bliss on the lounger under a towel.

When his fingers get in on the game, I come like crazy, yanking on his hair and calling his name. "Now, that's what I call an appetizer," Dex groans, as he finishes lapping up my juices.

Once he's done, he stands and kisses me. I moan when I taste my saltiness on his tongue, and it only gives me a craving for *him*. Reaching down, I unhook his belt and push down his pants and his boxers to free his cock. I fist it in my hand, working it over and tease it along my slit. "Later, I want this in my mouth," I mutter against his lips.

"Whatever you want, Miss Lexington. I'll never deny you."

"Will you fuck me now though?" As much as I want him in my mouth, I want him inside me more.

"Yes, ma'am." He slowly sinks into me, and my legs wrap around him tighter, pulling him in closer, deeper.

His lips possess mine, overtaking all my senses, as he thrusts into me. I'm at his mercy, entirely his. And to think a few months ago, I wasn't sure we would ever be *here*. Hopelessly in love…*and making love on my desk*…we've come so far and now I'm more than certain, I have forever loving this man.

Dexter lifts me off the desk, bouncing me on his cock, taking me harder and deeper. My whole body is tingling, and my stomach and core are clenching.

"You're right there, aren't you baby?" Dex mutters, and I mumble out something incoherent that resembles a yes. "That's what I like to hear." He recaptures my lips and thrusts into me faster.

Between the sounds of our moans, I make out the sound of my office door opening. "Fuck," I murmur under my breath, breaking away from Dexter's lips. I wrap myself tighter around Dex's body, peering at Kayleigh who is standing at the doorway looking at a couple of papers in her hands.

"Meadow, do you have the orders for Den—" Her eyes lift and instantly go wide. "Oh my god!" Kayleigh shrieks, and covers her mouth. "What are you doing?"

"What does it look like I'm doing? Get out!" I yell and point towards the door. Dexter sits me back on the desk and hides his head in my shoulder, laughing it up.

"Yeah, sorry." She shakes her head, flustered, but I see her peeking at Dexter's half exposed ass. Who is still painstakingly making short, sweet thrusts into me.

"Oh and lock the door too. Thanks." I smirk, and I swear I hear her mutter bitch under her breath, but I don't care. I'm so close at this point, she can bring everyone in to watch and I wouldn't care. The door clicks behind her as she goes.

"Oh shit…" Dexter groans, his forehead resting on mine. His thrusts suddenly stop, and I squeeze my walls needing him to move.

"What are you doing? Don't stop," I whine, tightening my legs around him.

"I want this to last, where you come so hard you forget your name." He tries to pull away from me, and I grip my fingers into his shoulders.

"I swear to god, Dex, if I don't come right now *and* our food gets cold, I *will* kill you," I grit out and then for good measure, I plaster on the biggest sugary sweet smile I can muster. I'm teetering on the edge of oblivion between innocence and crazed serial killer.

"Yes, ma'am."

He grabs my legs and tells me to lie back. I do as he says and fall back amongst the scattered papers on my desk. He lifts my legs, my heels now resting on his shoulders. He grips my thighs and plows into me. The papers around me go flying to the floor as I'm pushed back across my desk.

"Is this what you wanted?" he grits out and slams into me harder. Again and again.

I bite on the edge of my hand to keep myself from screaming and nod my head. He chuckles and reaches down, to play with my clit. But the second his thumb circles around my overly sensitive nub, I explode. "Fuck! Yes!" My eyes roll back in my head and my body quivers on my desk.

"Damn baby, I don't know if they heard you all the way over in the other building."

I try to swat at him, but my hand falls limp to the desk. Dexter's pace hasn't relented, drawing on the aftershocks of my orgasm. "You're squeezing me so tight," he groans, grabbing a hold of my thighs, and thrusting deep inside of me as he comes. "God damn." He breathes out, leaning down and kissing me softly on the lips. "Always fucking amazing."

"Mmm," I hum, at a loss for words for the moment.

He chuckles and reaches for one of the scattered papers by my head. "So, how's the Jacobson account going?"

"Not as good as this," I murmur, knowing nothing is ever as good as the two of us together.

"Good answer." He kisses me again and slowly drops my legs down.

He digs around in the bag of takeout, which managed

not to fly to the floor during our sexscapades, and pulls out some napkins. He cleans us up and then helps me sit up.

"I'm going to have to take advantage of you at your office one day." I grab his tie and place a kiss behind his ear.

"You're forgetting one thing, babe."

"What's that?"

"I have glass walls."

Oh yeah. Well...shit...

"Peep show?"

We settle onto the small couch in my office, our lunch spread out on the coffee table. I stab my fork into a juicy piece of orange chicken. I'm starving. Thank god for Dexter because I probably would've only eaten the candy bar I have in my desk for lunch.

"Hopefully, Kayleigh catching us doesn't affect your promotion," Dex says as I moan my appreciation for the delicious chicken that hits my taste buds.

I chew and swallow, shaking my head. "If she knows what's good for her, she *won't* say anything."

After Kayleigh took her little "vacation" she came back wanting to start over and appeared to be a changed person. She still is a bit of a stuck up snob, but she's been ninety percent easier to work with and no longer tries to sabotage me

Because if she does. She's not getting another chance from me.

"Plus, even if she did, I don't think Mr. Hanson would care. He was as bad as everyone else when he found out we finally got together. Even asked if he could help plan the wedding." I roll my eyes. I know it was mainly because it would look bad if I went with someone else instead of my own company to plan my wedding.

"Again, people always in this hurry to marry us off." Dexter chuckles and picks up a piece of his moo shu pork. "Don't they know we already practically are."

The topic of marriage reminds me of that conversation we had a while back about roommates. I bite my lip and wonder how Dex will take my news that I've been hiding from him for the last few days because I'm worried about how he'll take it. I didn't want to tell him before we left for our weekend because it's going to be such a huge change for us.

Huge.

"Hey, do you remember when you talked about the idea of getting another roommate?"

"I was just messing around with you." He leans over and kisses my nose. "I only want you."

"Oh, well, um...you see there might be a change in those plans now." I place my hand on my stomach and his eyes go wide, and his face goes deathly pale.

"What...what do you mean? Are you?" His finger points to my stomach. "No way."

"Am I what?"

214

I rub my stomach again, and I watch as his Adam's apple bobs in his throat. "Pre-gnant?... but how, though? I mean, it's too soon...isn't it?" He pauses, and his breathing gets heavier. "Unless, fuck! Your birthday. Holy shit." He counts on his fingers and looks to the ceiling, but I'm pretty sure he has no idea what he's counting.

I bite my lip, trying to keep myself from busting out laughing at his reaction, but it's priceless. He's freaking out and I haven't even said anything yet. He continues to stare at the ceiling, mouthing to himself and I guess it's time to bring him back to reality.

"Dex? Babe." I touch his knee. "Slow your roll."

His head pops back down at me, and he's still white as a ghost. "I wasn't ready for this. But okay. I got it. The house I wanted to build for us originally only had three bedrooms. Like that's enough, but then I got to thinking and that's stupid because what if we want more kids. I never really thought of kids before…"

My hand flies to his mouth and I cover it to keep him from talking. Now I'm sure *my* face is pasty white. "Is that what you were sitting there calculating?" He nods as I remove my hand from his mouth. "God Dex, I'm not pregnant, you crazy man. I went to the pound last week and fell in love with this dog and was hoping we could adopt her. Be pet parents. Now what the fuck is this about a house?"

"Gotcha!" He smirks and attacks me down to the couch and blows a raspberry into the side of my neck, making me groan and laugh.

"What do you mean, got me? You totally thought I was knocked up."

He grins and rubs his nose to mine. "Oh, I did for a second. Till you let out a little snort when you tried not to laugh."

"Damn. So…no house? It had started to sound good through your rambling."

"One day, I will design the house of your dreams. But let's get back to this new house guest. This *dog*. Is it bigger than my hand this time?"

"Yes, she's a Doberman. I've already named her Lady."

"Lady, huh?" He snorts. "We will see about that. Is this *lady* going to hate me?"

"Hopefully not. I want you to come down and meet her. She's *so* sweet," I gush.

I didn't *mean* to adopt a dog when I went to the pound on my lunch break last week. It just *happened*. I fell in love and put the paperwork in for her. She's not mine quite yet, there's still a few steps to fulfill before she can come home, but I hope she will be.

And if Dex says yes.

"Yes, but your idea of sweet dogs are ones that bite at my ankles and eat my shoes and piss on all my stuff." He raises an eyebrow and I laugh. Poor guy will be forever scarred by my pup.

"You loved Pickles. Stop it."

"I loved him because you did. That's all I'll defend. I'll come down and meet her."

"Really?" I clap my hands. "I promise, you'll love her."

He grabs my chin and plants a kiss to my lips. "I'm sure I will. Now let's get back to more important matters, such as, maybe it's time we only cohabit one room now."

"Why can't we keep taking turns? I mean we *just* started dating."

His eyes narrow into little slits. "*I* think it's time we make use of that third bedroom for what it's actually for."

The master bedroom. Instead of fighting over who got it, we had used it as the rental. Then when it wasn't being used, it became an office slash work out area.

"I don't know. Shouldn't we see if we like each other first, ya know, before we like live-live together?" I tease, wanting to egg him on because it's fun.

He rolls his eyes. "Seriously, Meadow?" He yanks me to his lap, and I straddle his hips. My nails trace up the side of his neck into his hair.

"Why does it matter what bed we sleep in, you have me—forever and ever. Remember? You made that lifelong commitment already when we were eleven. Sucker."

"Best thing I ever did." He kisses the corner of my lips, then my nose, then behind my ear. "But let's get back to the living arrangements. I've been wanting to buy a new, bigger bed. A king and it would fit best in the master, with *you.*"

"*Fine.*" I huff, but there's no real argument. Where else would I want to be than in the arms of the man I love and my best friend every night, in what would be *our bed*? Sharing a closet and the same shower. Sharing our lives…completely.

"I don't know what your huffing about. We'll need the extra room for our new dog child, won't we?"

A grin breaks out on my face and I press my forehead to his. "I love you."

"I love you, too." He flips me onto my back on the

couch, and I lose myself in the man that will always be my forever.

Epilogue

One year later...

Meadow

For my birthday this year, Dexter was loaned a massive house on a lake to celebrate. It was a thank you from one of his clients for the fabulous job he and Julian did designing the house last year.

I love the contemporary style of this house and all the large open windows that look out to the lake. Inside is a vast open floor plan, and everything is top of the line. I only hope Dexter knows when he designs our house, I'm going to have many requests from his past projects.

"I can't believe this house," I say in awe to Mel who is next to me on the patio overlooking the lake. The sun has set and the orange lights from the docks twinkle off the water.

It's positively gorgeous here.

The rest of our twenty or so friends are scattered

around inside the house drinking and partying away. This year, Dexter and I are limiting ourselves, so there's no chance of blackouts.

"I know. It's hard to believe sometimes that Dex and Julian *actually* design these. Like seeing them in person, fully finished. It's amazing."

"Speaking of *Julian*. What is going on with you and him?" Over the last couple of weeks, the two have been seen sneaking around with each other but they won't admit to anything other than just "hanging out." Then an hour ago, I caught them coming out of one of the bedrooms, and Mel was a little less than put together, with her hair a mess and her clothes disheveled.

"We're doing the casual thing," Mel says, shrugging, her cheeks slightly pink.

"Casual, huh? I didn't take you as a friends with benefits type of girl?"

"You only live once, I say, and he's *fun.*" She winks. "And he happens to like a little kink."

"I knew it," I laugh, smacking the banister. "Well, as long as you two are happy. I'm happy for you."

"We are. And don't worry, neither me or Julian are as clueless as you and Dex when it comes to our *feelings.* We know what we're doing."

"Ha Ha." I nudge her shoulder. "By the way, have you seen my boyfriend?" He disappeared about twenty minutes ago with Steve, Randy, and Julian. Now, as I glance inside I see the three guys standing around talking, but no Dex.

"Um—" Her lips twist, meaning she knows something, but before I can ask what's going on, Lady jumps on my back with a loud bark.

"Whoa!" I stumble a bit forward, but I'm able to catch myself. She barks at me, and then tugs at my arm, pulling me to the stairs. "Lady, what is going on?" I laugh, as she tugs on my arm again.

"Maybe Timmy fell down the well. You better go with Lassie there," Mel giggles, pointing towards the edge of the patio.

"Alright, girl. Take me to *Timmy*." I take a hold of her collar and she leads me down the steps. I'm led around the house, closer to the water's edge.

There's a small bonfire is set up and standing beside it is Dexter. His face glows from the embers.

"What are you doing down here all by yourself?"

"I wanted a moment alone with the birthday girl to give her her gift." He grabs my hand and yanks me into his chest. "But first..." His lips mesh to mine, kissing me so forcefully and possessively that it causes my head to spin. I moan down his throat and grip his shoulders as my legs go wobbly from this earth-shattering kiss that's conveying every ounce of his love for me. I'm unsure how much time has passed when he breaks away from me. "I love you."

"I love you too," I say breathlessly, inching towards his lips again. Wanting more. *Needing* more. Holy hell, do I want more of what that was. "Should we maybe go back inside?" I run my finger along his chest.

"Not yet. I need to give you your gift." He takes my left hand and kisses it.

"And you couldn't have given me my gift *inside?*" I huff.

I'm insanely turned on, and my sex is throbbing. Why couldn't that kiss be a part of my gift and the rest in bed?

"I wanted to be alone and romantic?" He gestures towards the little bonfire and the lake.

"Touché."

"I put one part of your gift on Lady's collar."

"Oh?"

Interesting.

"Go on. Take a look."

I call for Lady to come over and she trots over happily with her tongue hanging out. "Daddy says you have something for me." Kneeling beside her, I twist her collar looking for what could've been added. The only thing new is a pink dog tag. I lift it and can tell there's something engraved, but I can't make out what it is in the dark. "Dex, I can't read it."

A phone light casts over my shoulder, and as soon as I read the words; they steal every last bit of my breath and every beat of my heart.

Meadow, Will you Marry Me?

I drop the dog tag and my head spins to Dexter, who is now on one knee in front of me. The phone is now on the ground, illuminating the diamond ring in his hand.

"Meadow, you've been my best friend since we were in diapers and I plan to spend my life with you until we're in diapers once again."

"Oh my god...you didn't just go there." I laugh, but how could I expect anything less from this man?

"Of course, I did. I wanna grow old with you, Meow. Wrinkly, old and gray, and senile. I want to spend the rest of my life making you smile. Kissing your face and protecting you from harm. You're my favorite person and I love you so much, baby. So, Meadow Jane Lexington, will you marry me?"

"Yes, a million times, yes."

Dexter grabs my hand and slips the ring on my finger. "It's perfect," I whisper, admiring the white gold, princess cut, diamond ring that will now sit proudly on my left hand for a lifetime.

"Just like you, Meow."

I go to wrap my arms around his neck to kiss him, but before I can get my lips on his, Lady jumps on both of us, knocking us to the ground.

"Maybe one day we will get a normal dog," Dexter grumbles.

"Honey, we're not anywhere close to normal, our dogs won't be either. Now, where were we?"

Fourteen months later...

Dexter

Meadow and I are sitting in front of the Christmas tree at my parents' house wearing the most hideous ugly Christmas sweaters ever.

It's a tradition they said. It'll be fun, they said.

Translation: Let's add it to the wall of embarrassing pictures

"I think these are the worst sweaters yet," I groan pulling on the giant white fuzz ball on Santa's hat, who by the way, is riding on the back of a reindeer.

"I like them, they match your eyes." Meadow touches my cheek and leans in to kiss me.

"You're so full of shit," I whisper against her lips.

"Hey, there will be none of that right now. Let me get a picture of you guys in front of the tree. I need a new one for my mantel," my mother says holding up her camera. My dad stands beside her, biting his tongue, trying not to laugh at us. Something he's been doing since my mom made us slip on these repulsive outfits.

Lady comes running up and jumps on my lap, licking my face, not wanting to be left out of the family photo. "Settle, girl." I rub behind her ear, which makes her drool, but also calm down and she lies down in front of us.

"God, she's such a daddy's girl now." Meadow rolls her eyes, and I chuckle.

"That's only because somebody else has taken up all your attention lately." I place a kiss to her temple.

"Oh, my god. What was I thinking?" My mother stops the clicking of her camera. "We can't have a family picture without Wesley."

"No, we can't. So, I vote we take these things off till…"

"I have him right here." I'm cut off by Valerie walking into the room holding our two-month-old son. He's wearing a Santa Claus onesie and I'm totally jealous of my little dude. I would much rather be sporting the onesie.

"Bring my baby here." Meadow reaches out her arms. "I didn't hear him wake up."

"I might have picked him up, no longer wanting to wait to see the little guy." Valerie tries to look shameful, but we all know she isn't.

"Mom!" Meadow exclaims as she takes our son from her mother's arms. "I swear. I bet you didn't wake me up when I was a baby like this."

"Oh, hell no! I wasn't crazy. But it's also Christmas. Now take your pictures, so I can hold my grandson again before Joy hogs him."

"Me?" my mother argues. "Martha's the hog."

"Hey!" Aunt Martha stands from the couch, leaving Uncle Frank's side. "You can't blame me, he has the same little chubby cheeks Wes did when he was a baby."

Oddly enough, he does, compared to baby pictures. But also, so did I as a baby, but I don't say anything.

My father and Frank shake their heads and turn on the TV as the women playfully bicker. We are forgotten in our ugly sweaters on the floor, and little Wes falls back to sleep in my wife's arms.

I rub my finger down the side of my son's face and remember when I found out Meadow was pregnant with him. We were still two months away from the wedding when she came barging into my office one Thursday afternoon.

"I should kick your butt!" Meadow stands at the front of my desk, with her arms crossed over her chest. Usually, this stance would tell me I'm in trouble, but the goofy smile on her face is throwing her off altogether.

"And why is that?"

"Because thanks to you, I'm now going to have my wedding dress let out."

My head shakes, totally lost. "What are you talking about?" How am I to blame if she gained a couple of pounds? Though I have no idea where they are. She rounds my desk and straddles my lap. She's still grinning like a loon as she presses a kiss to each of my cheeks. "Meadow, I think you have successfully lost me, babe. What's going on?"

"Well, besides donuts and too many tacos what else could make me put on some weight?"

"I don't know? Too many margaritas and chicken wings?"

She rolls her eyes and sighs, annoyed. "Sometimes I wonder about you." Opening her purse, she pulls out a thin piece of paper and then hands it to me.

"What's this?"

"Look at it."

My eyes drift down to the four by seven paper in my hand. It's a black and white picture…

"No?"

"Yes." She nods her head vigorously and places her hand on her stomach. "We're having a baby."

A baby? I gape at her in amazement as I examine the sonogram. If it wasn't for the arrow, pointing at the sac telling me what it was, I might not believe it. After the initial shock wears off, I yank her to me and hug her tight. "I'm not sure if I could love you more."

"I'm taking that you're happy?" She giggles, throwing her arms around me.

"Happy? I'm ecstatic, baby. Fuck." I grab the back of her neck and pull her lips to mine. Ravishing her, tasting her, and never wanting to let go. My hand roams over her stomach, and it's hard to believe that I'm going to be a dad. We are going to be a family.

There's a loud knock on the wall of my office, making

us separate. We both turn to see Julian in front of the glass shaking his head at us as he enters the room. "I thought we talked about this."

"Sorry." Meadow flushes. "I had some big news I had to share with him that couldn't wait." She grabs the sonogram and shoves it back in her purse.

"Oh yeah?" He crosses his arms and looks between us, eyeing us curiously. "That good, huh? Where it looked as he was about to take you on his desk?" He chuckles softly.

"Yes. I got those little crab balls and the bacon wrapped scallops he wanted so badly for the wedding." Meadow smiles cheekily and gives me a wink.

"Mmm-hmm."

We were able to keep the pregnancy a secret till the wedding, announcing our little surprise at the reception— alongside those mini crab balls—And the moment we found out we were having a boy, there was no doubt in our minds that we wanted to name him Wesley James after our best friend. To honor him and always carry on his memory.

"Okay, you two let's try this again." My mom calls out.

"Hey," I grab her face and run my hand gently down her cheek, "I love you."

"I love you, too."

"Forever and ever…" we say together, kissing each other on the lips before turning to smile at the flashing camera.

The End

Erica Marselas

Bonus Epilogue

THE LOVE PLAN: MAKE LOVE TO ME
BONUS EPILOGUE CONTENT!!

It was originally written for this story and used in the Take Me to Bed Anthology

Blurb:

Meadow is a horny pregnant wife with a stubborn, cautious husband.

His heart might be in the right place when it comes to her pregnancy, but at the end of the day, she only has one goal in mind.

Get her husband to make love to her.

THE LOVE PLAN: MAKE LOVE TO ME
BONUS EPILOGUE CONTENT!!

It was originally written for this story and used in the Take Me to Bed Anthology

Blurb:

Meadow is a horny pregnant wife with a stubborn, cautious husband.

His heart might be in the right place when it comes to her pregnancy, but at the end of the day, she only has one goal in mind.

Get her husband to make love to her.

Stubborn: my husband, Dexter Greene, is the definition. I've known the man my entire life, and once he has his mind set on something, there's no going back. So why would I ever think he would change now?

Like when he *finally* realized we were more than just "best friends" and that he was in love with me after years of built up sexual tension.

He had to almost lose me before he recognized that we were meant to be. *Though that's a different story.*

I love my husband, *but* I think I might have to hurt him. Because if he doesn't change his stance soon on having sex with his crazy, horny, pregnant wife…Let's just say he's going to find himself in an early grave.

Alright, let me back up a little and calm my hormones. It's not that he doesn't want to have sex with me; he's just being overly cautious.

AKA stubborn. AKA pigheaded. AKA insufferable.

I'm thirty-six weeks pregnant with our second child and spitting nails horny. (In case you missed it.) My last pregnancy with our son, Wes, was a little *bumpy* at the end. I had developed preeclampsia at thirty-two weeks and then ended up going into labor at thirty-five weeks.

It had been when I passed out after my water broke that left Dex traumatized. He was at work when it all happened, and it was hours before he could get to me because he got stuck in traffic. Admittedly, it was scary, and I was lucky my mother was with me at the time and I made it to the hospital safely. In the end, Wes and I were fine and there were no complications.

I thought Dex was good after the shock wore off. He even talked with a therapist after it happened, as it brought back some old memories to the surface of when we were teenagers, and lost our best friend, Wesley. Whom we honored by naming our son after. But now, I'm seeing from his helicoptering ways that maybe the fear will always linger there.

I've tried to appease the crazy man by taking it easy. I went on early maternity leave, being able to work mostly from home overseeing the event planning business I had recently taken over. But was that enough? Nope. Dex has taken off work so he can watch over me. He wants me to keep my feet up, laze around till I'm as big as the house he had built for us.

Maybe some women wouldn't mind their husbands waiting on them hand and foot. I guess I wouldn't mind if there was an orgasm included. He's convinced himself, thanks to a misinformed Google site, that an orgasm will cause early labor. Since I was early with Wes, he doesn't want to take the chance—with anything.

"Meadow, there's proof that orgasms can set off early labor. It says so right here on this website," he said

to me as he pointed to his laptop as I laid in bed with my feet propped up trying to ignore him and his overbearing ways.

I'm planning on disconnecting the WIFI for spreading lies to his head. At this point, he might as well wrap me in bubble wrap. But what's the use?

I'm the prisoner, and he's the warden.

Speaking of the warden, while he is distracted in the shower, I'm making my great escape to the living room, tiptoeing, ever so slowly, hoping that no creaky floorboards can give me away. But it's our dog, Lady, who barks at me from our bed, selling me out.

"Meadow? Where are you going?" Dexter calls out, standing in the doorway of our bathroom.

"You're supposed to be on my team?" I hiss at the large Doberman, who has her ears pointed up innocently. Traitor. He's even made my pup into a guard dog.

And I was so close. My hand was on the knob.

Why me?

I sigh as Dex walks into the room, a white towel hanging loose around his waist.

This no sex thing is going to be the death of me because I can't remember when I was ever this horny.

If it's not bad enough that he won't touch me, he won't let me suck that juicy dick of his either. He's holding both our orgasms for ransom, and right now, all I want to do is rip that towel away and jump his bones.

Sexy, annoying, irritating bastard.

"I was going to get a drink, then maybe go mountain climbing afterward. You know, a normal Tuesday morning," I say smugly, wearing the smug smile to go with it.

"Don't be a smartass, Meadow. You know if you need anything, all you have to do is ask. You should be in bed, with your feet up, resting."

"No, I should be in bed with your dick inside of me." I stab my finger into his chest, with a little extra bite to my bark.

He chuckles and shakes his head. Well, I'm glad to see he's finding this humorous. At least when he dies at my hand, he'll do it, laughing. "Get into bed, Meow." He goes to grab my hand, but I move it away from him. If he thinks calling me by his little playful nickname for me will give him bonus points, he has another thing coming.

"No, Dexter. Stop it already. The doctor said I was fine."

"And she said the same thing last time—'till you weren't."

Yep, I think I'm going to kill him. Consequences be damned.

"Oh my God, Dex. Every pregnancy is different. You need to stop being such a worrywart. It's not a good look on you."

He steps closer to me and places his hand on my cheek. "Fine. But, let's not push it again."

I roll my eyes, moving his hand away. I'm tempted to bite the damn thing off.

"The only way I'm crawling back in that bed is if you're going to fuck me. If not, I'm going to get myself a drink. Then find Wes and cuddle up with him on the couch and watch cartoons."

He sighs "All right, but if I come out there and your sexy ass isn't planted on that couch, well…"

"Well, what? Punish me? Please do." I purr, darting my tongue over my lips.

"And don't go lifting Wes, he's too heavy." He says, scratching the nape of his neck, totally ignoring my seduction techniques.

"Yes, dear," I mutter, while sarcastically fluttering my eyes.

He bites the inside of his cheek and closes in on me. His pupils dilate and my heart skips a beat at his darkening lustful stare. He leans in and his fingers graze the side of my face. My lips part and I'm quickly overtaken by his fiery, possessive kiss. The scent of his aftershave washes over me, and I melt in his arms. I grab his towel and pull it off him.

My hand wraps around his cock, and I start moving up and down his length, feeling him grow harder in my palm.

Finally.

"Meadow," he groans, grabbing my wrist.

"Don't fight it, Dexter, I need you," I moan against his lips, ready to kiss him again when he jolts his head away and moves my hand from his dick.

"Dexter—" I let out an exasperated sigh, running a hand through my hair. My sex is throbbing in need, just from that one kiss, and, I'm being denied—again.

He swallows hard. "Baby, we can't."

"Yes, we can!" I stomp my foot, not caring if I'm acting like a petulant child. *Does he not know how badly I need him?* "The doctor didn't say anything about not having sex. YOU DID. I want you, and I know you want me. So, why do you push me away?"

"You know why," he says.

In a huff, I grab the door handle, swing the door open, and rush out of the room. I make my way to the kitchen and see my mother sitting at the breakfast bar with Wes. Dexter got up this morning, like every morning since he's been home, and got Wes ready for the day. All while I lay in bed and twiddle my thumbs.

"Good morning, Meadow." My mom addresses me as she stirs Wes' oatmeal. She's been coming over in the mornings to help with Wes and keep me company since Dexter has put me on bed rest. "I see your captor has let you out of your cell today."

I shake my head and walk to the fridge to get some orange juice. "He's driving me nuts!" I exclaim, having the urge to yank my hair out.

"Mommy!" Wes wiggles his tiny hands at me. I know full well he wants me to pick him up, but instead, I walk over to him and let him put his arms around my enormous belly. He looks exactly like his father; brown hair, which is spiked to match Dex's, same brown eyes, nose, and chin, but thankfully he hasn't picked up that stubborn gene. *Yet.*

"Hi, sissy. Come out so I can play with you," he whispers.

"She'll be here soon enough, Wes." I kiss the top of his head as he continues to talk to his sister.

"She'll be here sooner if you don't take it easy," Dexter says as he walks into the kitchen dressed in a black t-shirt and jeans.

I roll my eyes and trying my best not to snap because I know he means well.

But I think my hands around his neck would look good right about now.

"Daddy, sissy kicked me in the head." Wes giggles and rests his head on my belly again. And sure enough, the baby kicks.

"She did, huh?" Dexter walks over to us and places his hand on my belly. The baby kicks, saying her hi to her daddy, which radiates the biggest smile out of him. "She's kicking up a storm."

Dexter's hand remains as Wes goes back to eating. His stare bores into me. The sexual tension is palpable between us, and I bite my lip, begging for him to kiss me.

"You should be sitting down," he grumbles, and all the energy around us goes crumbling down to my feet.

I shove his hand away from my stomach, and

march to my office. There's so much I want to say, a lot of it starting with the letter f, but with Wes there, I restrain.

Yep, I'm going to kill him. Single motherhood here I come.

Catching a glimpse of my reflection in the window, I wonder if he doesn't want to touch me because of how big I am. My belly is huge, I have stretch marks out the wazoo, and I'm swollen *everywhere.*

The dam breaks and as tears pour down my cheeks. I push the door open to my office and fall to the couch I have tucked in the corner and succumb to my tears.

Seconds ago, I was horny and now I'm a sobbing mess. Stupid, stupid hormones.

Maybe if my husband loved on me like he used to I wouldn't feel this damn pathetic, my inner voice snarks.

"Meadow?" Dexter cautiously says as steps into the room.

I shake my head, trying to shake off the tears, but it's no use. "What?"

"Baby, what's wrong?" He sits next to me and puts his arm around my shoulder.

Seriously?

I narrow my eyes into slits. "You won't have sex with me. You won't touch me. You don't find me desirable anymore."

"Meadow, baby, that's not true. You know it." He brushes my hair away from my face.

"Oh yeah? Then prove it."

"Baby, you're the most beautiful..." I put a finger to his lips.

"Not with words. But you can use your mouth—somewhere—to show me." I wiggle my eyebrows and lean closer to him.

He grabs my wrist and places a kiss into my palm

before letting it down. "It's not worth the risk. We only have four weeks."

"There's no way either of us could go four *MORE* weeks without sex. And did you forget about the additional six weeks with *nothing*? That's forever." I groan, nibbling my bottom lip.

"Meadow, just stop."

"Stop telling me to stop! I'm used to having your hands all over me almost twenty-four hours a day for the last four years, and now, it's like I have the plague. Forget not doing it, but you barely kiss me. In our room is the first time you've done that in weeks. So, excuse me for wanting to feel desired."

His eyebrows knit into a frown. "I do want you, but I'm just being cautious. I don't want the baby to come early like Wes did."

"Sex wouldn't be the reason why. Women have sex *all* the time while pregnant and don't go into labor," I snap.

He runs his hands through his hair and looks at the ground. "Why do you have to push this?"

"Why do you?" I yell, and then close my eyes, knowing I'm letting my temper get away from me.

I take a couple deep breaths to steady myself. I don't want to fight with him, but he has to see that even though he's being caring, he's also being overbearing.

"You've been over the top for weeks, and I know your heart is in the right place, but you're driving me insane. You have to trust me to know that I'm not going to push it. I know when I need to stop. Trust me when I say sex isn't going to bring the baby early."

The baby kicks me in the ribs, hard, and I wince, grabbing my side. Dexter is quick on his feet and moving me to sit on the couch. "What's wrong?"

"Nothing, just a tiny foot in the ribs. She thinks they're a xylophone," I groan when she does it again.

Dexter puts his hand where the baby is kicking and pushes slightly, whispering for her to stop hurting mommy. Oddly enough, the little one seems to listen and stops *for now*. "At least someone listens to me."

"Do you not trust me to keep the baby safe?" I ask, remembering he didn't answer me.

"I do." He cups my face with his hand. "But Wes' birth was one of the scariest days of my life. I wasn't there to catch you. Then, when I saw you..." He tenses up, his anguish from the day flashes through his eyes, and I cover his hand with mine.

"I understand, but that was a different pregnancy. You're here with me now, and I just want you to relax a little bit. I promise I'm not going to do anything crazy, but if you don't let me breathe or move out of bed—I will end up hurting you." I smile.

"I'll try."

"Thank you."

He leans in to kiss me, and I respond instantly, pushing my tongue between his lips. Shifting my body, I move to sit on his lap, but he stops me.

"We're still not having sex," he murmurs.

"*Dexter*…"

"*Meadow*…"

"Mommy!" The scream of our little boy causes us to break apart.

"Wes!" Dexter and I both yell back, matching his excitement. He jumps on the couch and crawls into Dexter's lap.

"Play!" He points in the direction of outside. My mom comes into the room and we oblige him by going outside.

I'm woken up by male voices whispering and a cool breeze blowing on my face. *Crap, I've fallen asleep outside on the patio swing.* I don't think I lasted more than a few minutes of watching Wes running around before exhaustion took over.

"You're all crabby and anxious." The first voice belongs to Julian, Dexter's boss and one of our best friends. *"Meadow is all out of sorts, according to Mel. You two need to get laid. If she goes into labor, I think she's at a safe enough time—"*

"I'd rather not find out though," Dex growls, cutting him off.

"Okay, okay, I get it, relax. But, can I be honest?"

"What?" he snaps.

"I think Meadow is about to put her foot up your ass if you don't fuck her into tomorrow. And I'm not dealing with your irritable ass for the next however many weeks. So, do you, Meadow, and the world a favor and have sex with your wife."

"I'm about to put my foot up your ass if you don't shut up."

"God, you're so stubborn. I mean, it was you who preached to me when Mel was pregnant how good pregnancy sex was, and now you're throwing it away. What if this is the last time it happens?"

Dexter groans. *"I hate you right now."*

"Just trying to put it in perspective."

"Still hate you."

My eyes flutter open, and I stretch my arms above

my head. I yawn loudly, announcing to the two men that I'm awake.

I'm glad to have Julian on my side even if it was my best friend, Mel, who planted the ear bug.

"Julian. Hi, what are you doing here?"

His lips twitch upward. "Mel has sent me on a mission to save you from your captor."

"Are you really calling me that to everyone?" Dexter narrows his eyes on me, and a creep of guilt rises in my belly.

My cheeks heat up, and I shrug. "Sorry, but I've told you I feel under house arrest. I still love you… even at this time of insanity."

"See you both need time away from each other. It would be good for you," Julian offers, and I nod.

"Oh, yes, please. Take him. Keep him." I grin and stand from the swing. "Please!"

"I'm not going anywhere," Dexter grumbles.

I glare at him. "Yes. You. Are."

"No."

I close my eyes and take a deep, cleansing breath. "Julian, do you mind?"

He nods and walks out to the lawn to join Wes and my mother who are playing on the jungle gym.

I sit back down and put my hand on Dexter's shoulder. "I love you, and I love you for wanting to make sure me and the baby are safe, but you *can* get out of this house for a bit. I promise nothing is going to happen in the next couple of hours. You need a damn chill pill, and I need a moment alone before we kill each other."

My gaze flickers to his crotch, and I know there's one way to either get him to go or finally get what I want. My hand moves up his leg and rests on his dick. "I mean, unless you would rather do something else?"

His dick twitches under my hand, and I'm relieved

that no matter how tense things are between us, he still gets turned on by my touch.

He stares at me, my hand rubbing across his hardening bulge. "We could role play? Warden and prisoner? You could handcuff me?" I bat my eyes and watch him gulp. "I've been bad, haven't I?"

He grabs my hand, moving it away from his dick and gently kisses me on my lips. "I'll go if you promise to call me the second if anything happens and wait for me."

"I promise. Now go out, drink a beer. Clear your worried mind for a bit." I wrap my arms around his neck and bring my lips to his.

Night has fallen. Wes is tucked into his bed, sound asleep, my mom has gone home, and Dexter is still out with Julian. I'm finally alone with some peace and quiet. *And my sanity.*

Now there's only one thing left to do. If he isn't going to give me what I want—it's time for me to take it into my own hands. Because I *really* need a mother flippin' orgasm.

Every time I even get my fingers close to my core, he's there. I swear he has cameras on me or some kind of sixth sense on when his wife is about to masturbate. If he won't fuck me, fine, but he could give me the release.

I know he's getting off. Those long showers aren't just for getting clean. Yet, here I am suffering.

I grab my computer and go to my closet to find Mr.

B.O.B. Once I have everything I need, I crawl into bed and make myself comfortable, leaning against a bunch of pillows. I load my computer and find some good porn. I flip on the vibrator and make my way to my core.

I circle it around my clit, as I watch the man on the screen eat the girl out. I envision Dexter's tongue on me, and imitate what he would do, letting the vibrator run along my folds and again around my clit.

Pushing the vibrator inside, I move it in and out, now matching the thrusts of the man on the screen. I grab my breast and roll my nipple, and *ahh*. My eyes close and my head tilts as I enjoy the sensations and listen to the panting and the moans of the couple on the screen.

I pump it harder, needing more. I'm building, and my toes grip the sheets. Just when I think I'm going to get what I've been deprived of the angry voice of my husband makes it vanish.

"What are you doing?"

Busted. My eyes fly open to see Dexter standing at the door. He's glaring at me, but I can see his eyes dart to my pussy where the vibrator and my hand remain.

"What does it look like?" I ask, eyeing the sudden growth in his jeans. I move the vibrator again, craving the release. *He's not ruining this for me.*

His angry glare soon becomes dark and predatory as he inches closer to me. His shirt goes over his head, revealing that six-pack I love to drool over. I close my laptop with my foot, no longer needing it's entertainment, as Dexter undoes his belt. My mouth goes dry, staring at this man as the storm clouds in his eyes roll in.

I'm in trouble.

I really, really hope I'm in trouble.

His pants and boxers go next, freeing his hardened erection. I lick my lips, desperate to have him inside me again. He kneels on the bed between my legs and grabs his cock, working his hand up and down. I'm mesmerized watching him play with himself, and I move the vibrator faster, rubbing my achy clit.

I'm building again, and my eyes dart to Dexter's. The fire shooting from them blows away the storm, and I almost finish from the look alone.

"Stop," he growls.

Part of me what's to scream, 'fuck you,' while the other wants to know *just* what he wants to do to me. So, I do as I'm told, halting the vibrator's movements. A curve of a smile plays on his lips.

"Good girl." He reaches down, pulling the vibrator out of me, sending it buzzing to the floor.

He hovers over me and overpowers me with his kiss, making my body surrender to what he wants to give me. His dick brushes along my soaking folds. I sink my nails into his shoulders to try and keep myself upright.

"Do you need my cock, baby?" He murmurs against my lips. I nod, and he releases a chuckle from deep in his throat. "I need you to tell me, baby. You've spent all day doing so, and I know you can use your words."

I don't know where this sudden change has come from, but hell if I care.

"Yes, Dexter. I need you to fuck me. I need you to make me come."

A devilish smirk plays on his lips as he leans back into me, kissing the side of my neck, working his way down to my breast. He sucks on my nipples, hard, while the tip of his finger teases just barely inside my core. I thrust upwards, begging for more. I'm in bliss when he gives in; one, then two, then three fingers fill me completely, his thumb circling my clit. He nips on my breasts harder, making them ache.

God damn, I've missed his touch.

I'm whimpering in ecstasy as I build up again, and

if he doesn't let me blow—I really might hurt him.

"I should have never denied you, baby. You're so beautiful like this. Soaking my fingers." His hot breath tickles in my ear. "Your eyes closed as you bite your lip because you're so close. Your fucking moans." His fingers pump harder and my pussy grips around them, my whole body tightening up. "After you come, baby, I'm going to slip my dick into you and pound the shit out of you. Fuck you until you scream this house down."

His dirty talk is my undoing, and I unravel, gripping my hands into his hair, as I call out some version of his name.

He pulls his fingers out of me while I'm still trembling. I feel him move away, but it doesn't register until I hear his demanding, husky voice say, "Get on your hands and knees."

I manage to push myself up and maneuver on all fours, scooting to the edge of the bed where Dexter is.

"You look so sexy like this, baby." His hand runs over my ass, and then he gives it a slap.

"Mmm," I moan and wiggle my ass at him.

One hand grips my hip, while his dick rubs against my core. There's no warning, no 'ready baby,' before he slams into me, launching me forward. I grip the sheets, trying to keep myself up as he slams into me over and over again.

"Is this what you've been needing?" He pants out between each thrust.

"Yesss—" I cry, thrusting my hips back into him, desperately needing to meet his urgency.

"Oh, no, baby. I'm in charge right now." He holds my hips harder, stilling me, and takes back control. He arches me down lower, the hits now more urgent, hitting my g-spot each time. He's as bad as I am after a long period of no sex, and two and half weeks is like a lifetime for us, becoming a crazed wild animal in heat.

"Dexter…" I scream, not being able to hold on anymore, and come again, more forceful than the last one. My body turns to mush, and I'm finding it hard to stay up. Dexter is still ramming into me like there's no tomorrow. I turn my head, wanting to admire him. His eyes are closed tightly, his abs contract with each stroke, and the sweat dripping down them makes his skin glow.

Dexter's eyes open and he watches his dick move in and out of me. One of his many favorite sights.

"So fucking good," he groans.

"Mmm, yes, it is."

His eyes snap to me, catching me looking at him. I bite my lip, knowing just how it affects him. "Fuck," he murmurs and shakes his head. He's still holding back his release, but I know he's close. Managing to get back on my hands, I thrust back into him.

"Fill me, Dexter, I want you to fucking fill me with your cum."

His fingers dig into my hips, and with a gurgled moan, he comes deep inside of me.

I fall to the bed, on my side, trying to catch my breath. This was just what I needed. Dexter falls next to me and cradles me into his arms, kissing the side of my neck. "Thank you, Warden."

He lets out a deep chuckle. "Anytime, prisoner."

I made it to my due date. Right to the day.
Thank God.

Because honestly, every time Dexter and I had sex after that day, I was waiting for my water to break and for him to say, 'I told you so.'

Dexter sits on the edge of the bed beside me, holding our newborn daughter, Rain. She's absolutely perfect, and she looks just like me.

"Have I told you that even though you're an overbearing pain in the ass sometimes, I couldn't have picked a better father for my kids." I giggle, and run my fingers down the light stubble on his cheek.

"Even though you planned my murder a couple of times?" he asks.

"Even though."

He leans down to kiss me. His tongue parts my lips, asking for more, and I gladly give it to him, forgetting my hospital surroundings.

A loud moan escapes my throat, followed by someone clearing their throat.

Julian walks over and slaps Dexter on the back. "Congrats, man. I'm happy to see you made it to this point, *sated*, and Meadow's foot is not lodged in your ass."

"I'm going to kill you," Dexter grumbles, and Julian laughs before walking over to hug me.

"Congrats lady, she's perfect." He kisses my cheek and takes the baby from Dexter's arms.

While everyone is paying attention to our daughter, Dexter sneaks in another kiss. "I love you, baby."

"I love you, too."

There's a sudden mischievous gleam in his eye, and he leans in closer, his lips hovering over mine. "What do you say to maybe one more?"

I huff and shove his shoulder away. He laughs, and I know that's the reaction he was going for. "If I had the energy to move from his bed right now, I would stick that foot in your ass, Greene."

"Well, it's a good thing you can't move." He kisses me quickly before I can protest and goes to collect our crying newborn.

That man is really going to drive me nuts for the rest of my days. *Forever and ever.*

And I'm okay with that.

THE END

Check out my other titles on Amazon

YOU CAN STALK ME IN ALL THESE PLACES:

www.ericamarselas.com
Newsletter:

Facebook:@ EricaMarselas

My Author Group on Facebook:Author Erica Marselas

Instagram: @erica_marselas

Goodreads:

Pinterest Board.

ACKNOWLEDGMENTS:

To my husband: Thank you for being the most supportive person in the world as I take on this publishing journey. For taking care of the rugrats so I can write and also reading every chapter against your will. (HA! I'm just kidding.) At least till the point where you get annoyed with me because I ask you every hour if you read the last chapter. Love you.

To the best group of women I know: **Denise, Lexi, Leslie, Melissa, Aakriti, Paula, Suzan, Helen, Colleen, Q.B., Carmel, Harlow, Gemini, Kelsey, Kristen, Rose, Danielle J, Erin, Danielle, Hala, Kelly H, Kelly R, Kim, and Jeanette**. *I would be lost without you guys! Thank you guys for always having my back, listening to me, reassuring me, motivating me, and helping my stories grow. I owe you guys more then you'll ever know!!! Love ya all.*

To my readers: You guys are pretty flippin' awesome too. I love you guys. Thank you for coming along with me on this ride and enjoying the words I write. (then asking for more 😊)

ABOUT THE AUTHOR

Erica is a wife, a mother of four, and a tequila drinking smart mouth. When she's not wrangling her children and trying to keep them alive, she's writing. She'll write anything from steamy erotica, to HEA romance novels because not all love stories are created equal. As long as she can dream it, she'll write it.:)

Erica Marselas

Living The Dream Through Words

"Dreams come to us when we sleep—but when you write them down, they come alive."

This is the end 😊

Made in the USA
Monee, IL
15 January 2021